MONTENEGRO BOOK TWO

DARK SERENADE

ESTELA VAZQUEZ PEREZ

outskirts
press

This is a work of fiction. The events and characters described herein are imaginary and are not intended to refer to specific places or living persons. The opinions expressed in this manuscript are solely the opinions of the author and do not represent the opinions or thoughts of the publisher. The author has represented and warranted full ownership and/or legal right to publish all the materials in this book.

Montenegro Book Two: Dark Serenade
All Rights Reserved.
Copyright © 2017 Estela Vazquez Perez
v2.0

Cover image by 99designs. All rights reserved - used with permission.
Cover designed by Trif TwinArtDesign

This book may not be reproduced, transmitted, or stored in whole or in part by any means, including graphic, electronic, or mechanical without the express written consent of the publisher except in the case of brief quotations embodied in critical articles and reviews.

Outskirts Press, Inc.
http://www.outskirtspress.com

ISBN: 978-1-4787-8382-4

Outskirts Press and the "OP" logo are trademarks belonging to Outskirts Press, Inc.

PRINTED IN THE UNITED STATES OF AMERICA

New Orleans 1853

Mourning cries seep out of windows as howling winds circulate the decaying stench of death throughout New Orleans. Victor Montenegro walks the streets, which are deserted of the living, who still fear the plague and are weary of the sight of the dead sprawled on the cobblestones. It is October 13, 1853, and the board of health has officially declared the city free of the epidemic. Unlike the still fearful survivors who are sheltering in place, Victor strolls the streets, stomping his feet while carrying a gas lamp low to scare away the rodents that populate New Orleans, feasting on the orphaned corpses that have yet to be collected for a pauper's burial. Victor is searching for Suzette and Ivan, who are among the few brave souls out helping to collect the abandoned bodies. There are no new reports of yellow fever outbreaks and deaths from the plague, and therefore Victor is not concerned about becoming another victim.

Victor will survive the yellow fever plague of 1853, just as he will survive Henrietta's threat to bite him. Ivan has threatened Henrietta with desertion if she dares to turn Victor into a vampire. Angry with Ivan, Henrietta cries bloody tears as she too walks the deserted streets, snatching rats and putting them into her hand-carried steel cage. An immortal Victor is Henrietta's only hope to retain Ivan's eternal affection. Henrietta fears that if Victor dies, it will endear Suzette more to Ivan, which threatens Henrietta's place in Ivan's life.

As Henrietta rounds the corner of Royal Street, her lace dress floats over the bloated and decaying corpse of a man who died on his way back from interring his wife. She blinks the bloody tears from her eyes as she leans over and lifts a rodent from the side of the man and places it on top of the rodents in her crowded steel cage.

"Is my blood not enough, my love?" asks Drake.

Henrietta waves her hand over her face, and the bloody tears vanish. With smiling eyes, she turns to face Drake Forester, who is in human form.

"They are for the community, not just me. I love having your rich werewolf blood in my veins, but I do not want to drain you," Henrietta says sweetly.

Drake takes the cage filled with restless rodents and offers Henrietta his arm. Henrietta takes his arm and proudly walks with him; she thinks that the rodents will make a lovely offering for Ivan.

Victor removes his hat and dress coat. With respect, he hangs them on the praying hands of a six-foot marble angel. He picks up a shovel that was hastily abandoned, and he briskly walks toward Ivan to help. Ivan, illuminated by two gas lanterns, digs a grave. Ivan and Victor silently finish digging the fourth grave as Suzette arrives, sitting on a cart that is hauling the corpses of three men and a woman. Suzette is cradling a dead infant in her arms.

As Victor helps her off the coach, she looks over to the four fresh graves; with a hoarse throat, she requests, "Bury the woman with her child."

The reddish-pink hues of the sunrise stream down onto the

cemetery as Suzette's elegant coach approaches the gates. In silence, the three of them leave the cemetery and walk to the coach. As Victor and Ivan talk about meeting later that day for a couple of drinks before they resume collecting bodies for burial, Suzette caresses her horses, which, in respect for the town's dead, are adorned with black ostrich-feather plumes, their backs covered with black cloth. Suzette's black velvet cloak is dusted with grave dirt and the scent of death. As Suzette watches Ivan walk away to rest, Victor uncloaks Suzette, shakes off the dirt, and drapes it back over her shoulders.

As they travel through the town, the melodic sound of the horses' galloping on the cobblestones is disturbed by cries of the living. Suzette rests her head against Victor's shoulder, grateful that he is still among them. Victor can feel the heaviness in the air and the torment in her soul.

Caressing her hand that rests against his arm, he says, "My dear, after the last abandoned corpse is laid to rest, you and I should leave town. So much darkness all around us…it would be good to get away, spend a few days rejuvenating under the sun. Mexico has beautiful beaches and enchanting colonial cities."

Suzette does not respond. She has become light-headed, and she feels the threat of fainting in her stomach. Her immortal body is not ill, but her soul is fraught with worry. Victor, her mortal love, is unaware that she is a creature of the night and shuns direct sunlight.

"So much death around us. Death in itself is not tragic. What is tragic is being separated from your loved ones. We mourn our dead because we do not know if we will ever see them again. We all would like to believe that when our death comes we will once again be reunited with our loved ones. It is beautiful to hold on to that thought, but the reality is that purgatory and hell are full of souls. Death is beautiful. Death is the door to eternal existence, and though we will all walk through that same door of death, we will not all have the same destination," Victor says.

"Sounds like you accept death's will," Suzette says quietly.

"But I am not ready to depart this world. I survived the plague. I am not going to squander this blessing. While I never committed a mortal sin, I feel I need to do more, as I am in a position to help more than others. I have many blessings, and I need to show my gratitude in the hopes that when I walk through the door of death, I will be reunited with the Creator and my loved ones."

Suzette looks up at him, smiles lovingly, and says, "I will do everything in my power as a doctor and the woman who loves you to give you longevity."

After a light breakfast, Suzette and Victor retire to her bedroom. Both utterly exhausted, they soon fall asleep in each other's arms as the rising sun warms up the heavy window drapes.

The remaining abandoned corpses were laid to rest. The recent rainstorm washed away the decaying smell of the plague. Ivan and Suzette continue their trade as morticians to ensure their supply of fresh blood. As they drain the blood of a woman who died from old age in her sleep, Suzette expresses relief to Ivan that the woman had a long life and that her passing was peaceful. Ivan smiles at Suzette. With the plague now behind them, Ivan's and Suzette's lives are settling back to their usual routine of running their respective plantations, with Suzette practicing medicine and helping the Ursuline nuns. Ivan welcomes into town his fellow merchant marines and continues to hunt for treasures. Their lives are gratefully back to the rhythm before the plague, with one exception. Suzette honors her love for Victor, and out of respect for him, she will not be intimate with Ivan. It tortures Ivan to fight the desire to express his love to Suzette. The vampire monstrosity prevents mutual love. The Amare trance is the closest vampires can come to mutual love, and not once since becoming intimate with Victor has Suzette requested Ivan to put her under the Amare trance. And Ivan has not asked Suzette to allow him to put her under the trance because it would not be at the same level of intimacy now that Suzette is in love with Victor.

Victor's struggle to fall in love painfully remains. Victor feels that discovering his ex-fiancée in the arms of her true love has crippled his heart, preventing him from ever loving again. Victor loves Suzette's passion for life and her intellect, dedication to medicine, charitable spirit, beauty, and refined elegance. Victor is enthralled by her, but he is not in love with her. And he prays that, with time, his heart will recover, and he will fall in love with the woman who deeply loves him—Suzette. However, his relationship with Suzette racks his spirit, and he believes it is caused by guilt from not being able to return her love. Victor considers himself undeserving of her passion. Victor also feels for Ivan, who has been a true gentleman to him despite being in love with Suzette. Victor appreciates and respects that Ivan continues to bestow the gift of his friendship and partnership. Victor is comforted with knowing that Ivan finds solace in the loving arms of Henrietta.

Henrietta's dream has been realized; with Victor still in Suzette's life, she now is the sole proprietor of Ivan's affection. Henrietta takes care to never refuse Ivan's desperate need for her company when his heart aches and his longing for Suzette overwhelms him. It boils Drake when Henrietta neglects him when Ivan seeks her attention. Drake struggles with accepting the retribution of unrequited love for falling in love with a vampiressa, and he despises Henrietta's love for Ivan. On each full moon, vampires from around the world visit Wolf Tower to consume werewolf blood. Drake resents that he must extend the full-moon truce to Ivan when he visits Wolf Tower, for the sake of the economic well-being of his community.

Victor refuses to contemplate the day when he will depart from New Orleans and put miles between him and Suzette. Victor cannot phantom nourishing a long-distance romance. His place is in California, and Suzette is well rooted in New Orleans. Victor feels it would be cruel for him to even suggest to Suzette that she should leave her beloved community, which depends on her, and leave Ivan, who will suffer the loss of their special bond. Victor cannot bring himself to ask her to desert her plantation and the slaves she protects to follow him to California without the promise of love.

The Perished *Ana Luisa* Fleet of 1715

Ivan fills Victor's glass with more rum. Victor is grateful for Ivan's relaxed spirit. Ivan's camaraderie toward him is without question. Still, Victor's inability to look his friend in the eyes without the aid of rum causes him to feel regret.

"I gave you my word that I would commission a crew to search for the Spanish fleet *Ana Luisa*," Victor reminds Ivan.

It is now the end of November, and winter is diminishing the threat of hurricanes. A hurricane in 1715 furiously pelted the *Ana Luisa* fleet, striking it down to the depths of the ocean. The fleet's eleven ships entombed within them massive treasure, the likes of which were never again duplicated.

In his soul, Ivan feels that the reason the *Ana Luisa* has never been found is not due to the lack of commitment or the technique of the countless treasure hunters but the result of an unworldly reason he has yet to discover. It is November, and, yes, the threat of hurricanes is diminishing, but the urgency in Victor's manner points to something else.

"Do you have plans for the holiday season?" Ivan casually asks Victor.

Victor takes another card from the deck and throws it up into midair, between him and Ivan, and with a flash, the card disappears in front of Ivan's unfazed eyes. Victor throws up two more cards, watching as each one vanishes with a blinding flash. Victor then looks down at his deck of cards and answers, "I must visit my family for the holidays, or I risk getting disowned."

Ivan smiles at Victor and then takes a card from the deck in Victor's hand. Ivan shows the card to Victor, then he throws it up between them, and the card freezes in midair. Ivan snaps his fingers; the card becomes engulfed in flames and then disappears. Victor's astounded eyes stare at the smoke left behind by the vanished card, and he asks, "How did you do that? Where did you learn to do that?"

Ivan humbly smiles and answers, "A magician never tells. It is a trick I learned from an illusionist who boarded my ship, but he did not survive the voyage."

Victor smiles at him, still astounded.

"Perhaps one day I will share that trick with you. And you will see that the true illusionist is you," Ivan says.

Ivan, ignoring Victor's confused eyes, reaches for the bottle of rum, fills their glasses, and then raises his cup to Victor and happily says, "Here's to us finding and claiming the most beautiful treasure that has seduced countless men on this planet, the *Ana Luisa*."

Once every third year, the harvest moon appears in November. Ivan stands alone on the shore, his dark cloak billowing behind him. The tides crash in as he looks at his pocket watch. It is three minutes before midnight, and the sound of the ocean rings loud in his ears. The ocean mist is welcoming, and he is hopeful that this harvest moon will illuminate his hunt for the *Ana Luisa*. The strength of the balmy winds hints to a hurricane building out at sea. At midnight, his vampiric senses will be heightened. At midnight, the ocean will tell him her secrets. The harvest moon grows, bigger illuminating the crushing waves. He looks at his pocket watch; it is now midnight. His vampiric eyes look up at the moon, which is now even fuller. The ocean becomes still, and the winds vanish. He morphs into a bat; guided by the illuminating moon, he flies over the ocean as he employs his vampiric bat echolocation, heightened by the full moon. At the horizon, his echolocation hits strong metal and dense wood. He hovers over the area as he morphs into a human being with bat wings to hold him over the ocean. The ocean then stirs violently and releases the scent of gold. Under the overwhelming moon, the ocean becomes still and clear as glass. Spilled jewels from the *Ana Luisa* hidden for centuries shine and glimmer beneath the sea. Ivan smiles, he has found the most coveted and revered treasure in the history of the world.

The Haunted Sea

Victor does not question how Ivan located the feverishly sought *Ana Luisa*. Victor will keep his word and commission the expedition to recover the lustrous treasure. Victor yields the authority of the recovery to Ivan. Victor trusts the seasoned merchant marine and treasure hunter to assemble an experienced crew and select the biggest ship for the historical recovery. Victor will pay the crew and rent the ship; in return, he will keep the treasure he hoists up and be part of the treasure's history.

Victor dives into the ocean after Ivan plunges in. The bottom of the sea is dark and still. Victor is confounded by the lack of sea creatures. Victor looks ahead to Ivan, who is standing at the bottom of the sea, staring through the water. Disappointment flows through Victor; the mighty treasure is not in sight. Victor's need for air is becoming urgent, but Ivan's still posture alarms Victor. Ivan is standing unchallenged by the sea's current. Ivan's attention is mesmerized by a vision that Victor's eyes cannot fathom. Victor swims to Ivan to boost him back up for air. Victor touches Ivan's arm, and a world materializes before Victor's eyes. The seabed is sprinkled with confetti jewels glistening under the countless fire torches situated between eleven mighty ships. Captivated by the scene, Victor does not realize that his lungs are not taking in water.

Without removing his eyes from the incredible treasure, Ivan says to Victor, "Behold the treasure we seek; it has sunk into another realm."

"Welcome to the devil's seabed," bellows a voice from the deck of the most legendary ship of the *Ana Luisa* fleet, the *San Esteban*. The voice chills Victor's soul and revives him from his stupor. Victor looks to the deck of the coveted *San Esteban*, and he sees a towering figure, elegantly dressed in attire from the early eighteenth century. The figure's tricorn hat conceals his face.

"Pirate Goldendeath," Ivan says angrily.

"Captain Goldendeath," Goldendeath corrects Ivan.

"Captain," Ivan mocks him with an incredulous tone.

Captain Goldendeath looks up from underneath his tricorn hat, and his ghastly skull mortifies Victor. Goldendeath relishes the shock in Victor's eyes, and he taunts him, "Congratulations, Señor Montenegro, you've discovered another underwater city."

"We are here to claim the *Ana Luisa*," Ivan states.

Victor focuses on his senses. There is no demand for oxygen from his lungs. He can feel the water swirl around them like air. His eyes scan the vision before him. The centuries-old eleven ships, beautifully preserved, are sitting majestically as if they are waiting for their maiden voyage. Precious gems and gold coins unmarred by the ocean pave the paths between the ships. A treasure hunter's aspiration.

Guttural laughter from Goldendeath pulls Victor's eyes away from the unbelievable vision, and Victor turns to face the ghastly skull of Pirate Goldendeath.

"You cannot claim her, immortal ghoul," Goldendeath belts out to Ivan.

Victor's astonishment at being able to hear underwater is replaced by his horror at Goldendeath referring to Ivan as an immortal ghoul.

"On whose authority can I not claim the *Ana Luisa?*" Ivan demands.

"The devil himself, Señor Ortiz." Goldendeath calmly reports.

"Why are you not in hell?" Ivan demands.

Goldendeath's laughter causes the ocean to shift around them.

"I am glad you asked. I made a deal with the devil. From time to time, I am allowed to escape the lake of hell to mine for souls. You see, the devil has an unquenchable lust for blood." Goldendeath smirks at the angry Ivan and continues, "The devil's lust for blood is never ending, as you, Ivan, can perfectly understand."

Victor's attempt to awaken his spirit from the horror is to no avail. Victor tells himself that this is a nightmare as he looks at Ivan, wanting to understand his lust for blood.

Goldendeath spreads out his skeletal arms and proclaims, "The devil claimed *Ana Luisa* for himself and docked her in his underwater realm. I am *Ana Luisa's* steward."

"Why the *Ana Luisa?*" Victor demands.

"Stupid question, Montenegro, but I'll humor you. *Ana Luisa* is the most coveted fleet in the history of mankind. Her treasure has claimed many lives, and yet men still lust for her. Her whole crew perished with her and now are sentenced to this realm. The devil uses the lust for the *Ana Luisa's* treasure as a beacon to claim more souls. *Ana Luisa* sank, but she was never abandoned. Her crew is still here, unable to let go of her jewels."

A small army of pirates comes into view; their gallant attire does not deflect the monstrosity of their bodies, caught in a perpetual state of decay.

Victor's desperation at the thought of being unarmed is quickly replaced by his horrific realization that arms will not protect him from the devil or his demons.

Ana Luisa's ghouls crowd closer.

"Hellish demon," Ivan curses at Goldendeath.

Ivan looks at the bewildered Victor with concern, and then Ivan announces, "We shall retreat from your hell, Captain."

Guttural laughter from the crew rocks right through them.

"Permission granted. Your condemned immortal soul has no value for me. However, Montenegro's soul is worth the weight of his body in gold," Goldendeath says gleefully.

"Montenegro leaves with me," Ivan fires back.

Goldendeath lifts his leg and places it on top of one of the ship's guns. He leans forward, and in the tone of a stern father, he ridicules, "What part of mining for souls did you not understand? A soul is my get-out-of-hell key. There is not enough horror and terror in the world to adequately depict even one-tenth of the horror and terror in hell. There is a war going on, gentlemen. A spiritual war. The devil has declared war on God, and the devil wants more souls in his domain. The devil is a capricious tyrant with a power second to God's, and he is relentless as a fisher of men. Men are weak and easily seduced, but there is still much good in the world, and that infuriates the devil. You can say he holds a grudge. This is not a game; still, he will play so that he wins. Montenegro is my ticket out of hell. If he parts with his life, back to the lake of hell I go."

"Not as mighty and fearless, Captain Goldendeath," Ivan growls.

"Unlike you, I face my demons," Goldendeath snorts.

On each side of Goldendeath, a dog materializes. The dogs are the darkest black Ivan and Victor have ever seen. Their pupils are fires from hell; when they growl, their dark leather bat wings expand.

"Meet my pets! They are dogs from hell. Like the devil and Ivan, they thirst for blood," Goldendeath says with utter glee.

Victor's mind is swimming with horror and dismay.

"Keep those demons on a leash, Captain!" Ivan demands.

Goldendeath's laughter chills Victor.

"My demon dogs are thirsty. They have not had a drop of blood in a century. They are very thirsty, my pets. Their bite sentences their victims to the realm of the undead, where the victims will be terrorized into submission to do the devil's work as they die. But, alas, it is a slow and agonizing death. Victims suffer pain, psychological terror, and hellish visions of being the devil's stepping stool."

As chilled as Victor is by Goldendeath's words, he refuses to believe the world he is in. He does not believe his vision any more than he believes he can breathe and hear underwater. He believes he is experiencing a surreal nightmare that he will soon awake from.

The responsibility for Victor's safety falls on the shoulders of Ivan. Ivan knows that it is not a vision; he knows that they dove into the devil's seabed. In a flash, he now understands why the *Ana Luisa*'s treasure has never again been seen above water. And why the countless souls, over the centuries, who attempted to boost it, to be the ones who found the *Ana Luisa*, were never heard from again. Ivan's heart sinks at the thought of having to tell his true love, Suzette, that Victor was not only lost at sea but that his soul was kidnapped by the devil himself. No, he will not allow it.

"I would love to split a bottle of rum with you chaps, but the devil is impatient." And with that, Goldendeath releases his demon dogs. One attacks Ivan solely for his blood. The other attacks Victor for his soul as it quenches its thirst.

The pain of the dog's horrendous fangs shoots throughout Victor's body, forcing him to try to tear the vampire dog off his neck. But the hellhound's teeth are locked in, and the more that Victor tries to pull him off, the stronger his bite and suction become.

Ivan suffers the same pain as Victor. But he is desperate to free himself of the vampire dog so he can save Victor's life and soul. Ivan instinctually knows that the demon dog will not let go of Victor until he sucks half of Victor's blood, and then he will be left to slowly die a painful death as he is spiritually tortured from the cursed bite. The job of the demon dog that is latched on Ivan's neck is to suck him dry until he is in a zombie state. Ivan grabs a broken oar and puts the pieces together to make a cross. He presses the cross against the body of the demon dog latched on his neck. The cross burns into the dog's side, and the demon dog, in utter agony, releases Ivan from his bite and retreats, trembling with pain. Taking care to keep the cross away from his own gaze, Ivan holds the cross in front of him. At the sight of the cross, the ghastly crew fall to their knees and bow their heads in sorrow and shame. Goldendeath lowers his tricorn hat and disappears. Ivan runs to Victor and presses the cross against the vampire dog that grips Victor's neck, and it releases him. Still thirsting for blood, the two demon dogs attack each other. The blood from the feuding dogs and from Ivan's and Victor's necks transforms the water into a blinding crimson.

Ivan fights to keep his strength. He places Victor's arm over his shoulder and, still clutching the cross, uses his echolocation and the buoyancy of the sea to hoist them up. His ship is nowhere in sight. The superstitious crew fled when they saw the blood in the water.

With the little strength he has left, Ivan drags Victor onto the shore. The vampire dog sucked half of his blood, and Ivan feels his flesh sink against his bones. Victor is in agony, contemplating his slow death and struggling with diabolical visions. Hoping that he will be heard, Ivan telepathically sends out a distress call.

A distant silhouette against the full harvest moon starts to move closer to the shoreline. Recognizing the outline of the coach gliding toward them, Ivan is grateful his call was heard, and he leans back against the bloody, wet boulder. A handsome black coach with a team of black horses wearing black plumes comes to a stop six feet before Ivan and Victor.

"What demon did you escape from?" the driver of the coach asks as he glides down to them.

Ivan gratefully looks at his fellow vampire and answers, "Vampire dogs."

The vampire, using his hand like a maestro of a symphony, raises Victor and Ivan into the coach.

———•((()))•———

The desperate pounding on her door startles Suzette. She pushes away her accounting book. Fearing for their safety, she orders the help not to open the door. Suzette swings the door open to find Ivan, grotesque and weak from lack of iron, doing his best to hold up Victor, who is showered in blood. Suzette yells for Maximus. The vampire coachman lifts Ivan over his shoulders. Maximus throws Victor over his shoulders. They rush to the plantation's lower-level morgue. The help, not liking the company of the dead, as usual, do not go down to the morgue. Ivan is placed on a chair, and Victor is rolled out onto the morgue's slab.

"What the hell happened?" Suzette fearfully asks as she fights tears.

"Demon dogs," Ivan sputters.

"Please hurry—locate Henrietta and tell her to get here quickly!" Suzette pleads to the vampire coachman.

Maximus slashes his wrist and begins to feed Ivan to prevent him from morphing into what vampires fear most: a hideous creature void of any human likeness in the state of a zombie.

Suzette leans over Victor. Victor is tormented by unbearable physical pain and suffering a fever as hot as hell's flames. Suzette bears the burns on her hands as she touches him to try to console him. When he is able to escape his hellish visions, he prays for life. Suzette's heart shatters as she watches Victor suffer his slow and torturous death sentence.

With her bat wings still visible on her back, Henrietta rushes into the morgue. Her eyes try to make sense of what she is seeing.

As she rushes to Ivan's side, she looks up to Maximus for answers.

"Demon dogs," Maximus says, tired from having given his blood.

Henrietta grabs a knife from a tray on a nearby table, and she slashes her throat. She sits on Ivan's lap and presses his head against her open skin, and he begins to drink. As Ivan feeds off her, Henrietta looks to the morgue's slab, and she is horrified by Victor's torture. For once, Henrietta feels pity for Suzette.

The blood from Maximus and Henrietta quickly restores Ivan's health and appearance. Ivan kisses Henrietta's hand; he then gently pushes her off his lap and walks to stand by the inconsolable Suzette.

"Is there anything that can be done to make his suffering less? A spell to ease the pain and torment?" Ivan asks.

"Medicine or magic cannot prevent his death and suffering," Suzette says, sobbing.

"You are just waiting for him to die?" Henrietta demands.

"What can be done?" Maximus insists.

In a lucid moment, Victor grabs Suzette's hand, and he implores, "I do not want to die, I do not want to be a stepping stool for the devil. I do not want to die miles away from my family. I want to see my family."

"My love, medicine cannot help you. I promise you I will always love you, and I will pray night and day for the rest of your soul."

"Rest for his soul—there is no rest in hell!" Henrietta yells.

"Henrietta, please do not mortify Suzette," Ivan pleads.

"Save me from the grips of hell," Victor begs.

Henrietta paces around, and then she walks over to the slab. She lowers her head to Suzette's head level. She glares at Suzette over Victor's waning body, and she clearly demands, "Save him from hell and give him everlasting life."

"I will not condemn him!" Suzette says in agony.

"He is already condemned to hell, my dear."

Suzette's sobs grow louder as her blood tears rain down onto

Victor's bloody body.

"I will save him!" Henrietta declares.

Ivan pulls Henrietta away from the slab and wraps his body around her to keep her away from Victor.

"Save him!" Henrietta shrieks.

Victor opens his eyes and looks straight into Suzette's eyes, and he begs, "Save me."

"As a doctor, my love, I cannot save you. All I can do is offer you everlasting life."

"Keep me away from the gates of hell so I can see my family again."

"He is delirious. He does not know what you are offering," Maximus warns.

"The choice is clear, hell or life!" Henrietta yells.

"I can send for a priest. Perhaps he can banish his demons, and give him last rites so his exit from this world is less painful and more peaceful," Ivan solemnly offers.

Suzette reluctantly nods in agreement between sobs.

Henrietta, furious, strikes Ivan hard in his stomach with her elbow.

"You are all selfish cowards. Send for a priest? That is your solution? When we have the power to keep Victor on this earth, so he can see his family and fight for his soul?" Henrietta says.

In another moment of lucidity, Victor grabs Suzette's arm, and he demands, "If you have a way to keep me on this earth so that I can see my family and fight for my soul, do it!"

"Do it!" Henrietta echoes.

Suzette, conflicted, looks at Victor. His suffering is great. A human body is not build to withstand the injury he suffered. The loss of blood would have been enough to kill him, let alone the terrorizing pain. While Suzette as a doctor wants to end his pain, she is more concerned for the salvation of his soul.

"Victor needs to be condemned on earth in order to keep him out of hell?" She questions.

"Victor is not a murder or a thief. Victor is not a bad person. He does not deserve to go to hell as payment to the devil so that Goldendeath can get a furlough from hell," Ivan concedes.

"Yes, Victor deserves to fight for his soul before he is locked in hell," Henrietta argues.

"I need more blood," Suzette requests.

"I will find blood," Maximus says as he hurries out of the room.

Victor thrashes about on the slab, tormented by agonizing pain and vicious hallucinations. Suzette looks up at both Ivan and Henrietta, and she laments, "His body will survive, his soul, imprisoned in his body, will escape hell, and his heart will never again know mutual love."

"In hell, love does not dwell," Ivan says.

"On earth, he can still fall in love," Henrietta says.

Suzette cups Victor's face with her hands, and she says, "I am going to give you immortal life so that you can fight for the salvation of your soul."

Suzette caresses the side of the neck that was not mauled by the devil's vampire dog. Ivan steps back and turns away. Henrietta takes a few steps closer and keeps her eyes on Suzette, who is standing over Victor.

As blood tears cascade down her ghastly gray face, she unleashes her fangs and bites Victor's neck. Henrietta smiles. Ivan paces with his back to them.

Victor's blood streaming into Suzette revitalizes her body as her soul aches. Suzette straightens up, her eyes fixed on Victor.

Guttural growls escape Victor's chest as the demon of pain, demon of hallucinations, and demon of torturing death exit his body, leaving behind the smell of rotting flesh in their wake.

Henrietta covers her mouth and nose with her cloak as she walks back to stand closer to Ivan. The angry and evicted demons are a heavy reminder to Ivan as to how dark is his world.

Peace cloaks Victor's face. The brutal gash quickly closes and heals. Before their eyes, Victor quickly transforms into his former self but is severely dehydrated.

Maximus quickly enters, holding in each hand a glass jug filled with blood. Suzette studies the jugs. Maximus informs her, "Mixture of rodent and vampire blood from the vampire coachman."

In a dehydrated stupor, Victor sits up from the slab reserved for the dead. "I do not feel like myself, and I am incredibly thirsty," Victor says to Suzette.

Maximus hands him a jug. Victor, too thirsty to examine the jug, gulps down the blood as if it were fresh water. Victor releases the empty jug, and it crashes to the floor. Victor takes the other jug and drinks it just as quickly.

Silence fills the room as they all watch as Victor's sunken skin becomes hydrated.

No longer tormented by pain, thirst, and evil hallucinations, Victor looks around, bewildered. He then turns and looks at Suzette and Ivan.

"What is the last thing you remember?" Ivan asks Victor.

Victor looks at Ivan's uninjured neck, and he confusedly states, "I am having a nightmare."

"It was not a nightmare, brother," Ivan says.

Victor looks at Suzette; the torment in her eyes rocks him.

Victor turns to Henrietta, and the memory of her demanding that he be saved hits him. He looks down at the hard and cold slab he is on. Victor jumps off and demands, "What the hell happened?"

"Perhaps we should go upstairs and talk about it," Maximus suggests.

"No, I do not want the staff to overhear," Suzette says.

Against the wall, there are two long sofas for the use by family mourning their dead.

"Let's sit down," Suzette says as she looks at the sofas.

"Thank you, but I'd rather stand," Victor says.

He studies Suzette's pale face that is streaked with red tears. Suzette lowers her head.

Victor turns to look at Ivan, and he demands, "Tell me about Goldendeath."

Ivan straightens his posture, and he begins, "Goldendeath was an infamous pirate whose mission was to own all the gold in the western hemisphere. The bodies he left behind, in his unmerciful quest for gold, are estimated to be in the hundreds. Goldendeath was feared even by the cruelest pirates because his brutal killing sprees never left a scratch on him. Two centuries ago, off the coast of Cuba, Goldendeath jumped onto the ship of his rival, Pirate Thomas Morris. Goldendeath wanted Morris's trunk of gold, and Goldendeath did not like that Morris was as infamous as him and almost as feared as he was. Goldendeath's mission that late afternoon was not just to confiscate Morris's gold; he wanted Morris dead. Goldendeath and Morris ordered their respective crews to stand down. Goldendeath and Morris both wanted to go down in history as single-handedly destroying the other. It was an epic sword fight. Before the wounded Morris hit the deck, with the last strength in him, Morris swung his sword and decapitated the overly confident Goldendeath. The respective crews were stunned that Goldendeath's headless body remained standing as his head rolled to his feet, then looked up at his body. One man bellowed, 'Goldendeath is the devil—that is why he is still standing.' Morris ordered his terrified crew to throw Goldendeath's body and head into the ocean for the sharks to feast on. Seven days later, Morris died from the wounds left by Goldendeath's sword."

Henrietta giggles, and then she chimes in, "Fools! There are plenty of riches, but only one life."

The shock on Victor's face is painful for Suzette; she sits down and keeps her eyes on her feet.

"Goldendeath continues to live, still surrounded by riches, but his true treasure—his soul—now belongs to the devil," Ivan says.

Victor's hand examines his neck.

"The reason I found the *Ana Luisa* on this hunt was because you were with me. Believe me when I tell you that I had no idea this would occur. Nobody did. Throughout the decades, those who hunted for her never returned from the sea to warn anyone. I felt it was a coincidence that they all perished at sea. But it was not. Goldendeath is no longer hunting for gold but souls," Ivan says to Victor.

"Demon dogs—it was not a nightmare," Victor says.

"I found a broken oar that I fashioned into a cross to get the demon dogs off our necks."

The shadows in the room grow, and the lingering smell of rotting flesh is not as overwhelming as the silence as Victor desperately tries to make sense what is going on.

"This is a dream within a dream," Victor declares.

"Do you not smell the rotting flesh?" Maximus asks solemnly.

"Why am I still here?" Victor asks. Victor then looks at Ivan, who is studying him, and he asks him, "Why are you here?"

"The reason why I found the *Ana Luisa* is because you were with me. Your soul was not damned," Ivan says with regret.

"A demon dog's attack sentences its victim to a prolonged and excruciating death. Once dead, the victim's soul becomes the property of the devil. You are still here because you begged for salvation so that you could see your family and work to save your soul."

"I? We were both attacked," Victor says, confused.

"Ivan is already condemned. This is why the devil did not let him find the treasure. The devil opened his realm because you, a mortal man, were with him," Henrietta explains.

Victor looks at them with confusion and a desperate fear. Suzette trembles, fearing Victor's reaction. Maximus looks at Ivan, waiting for him to expose them all for who they are.

"We are all vampires," Henrietta announces.

Victor looks at Henrietta, utterly stunned.

"Well, Maximus is a werevamp—half werewolf and half vampire," Henrietta adds.

Suzette's furious eyes glare at Henrietta.

"Be done with it. We cannot drag this out another century without him noticing," Henrietta smirks.

Henrietta looks at Victor, and she discloses, "The vampire who is desperately in love with you saved your life and soul by giving you immortal life. Know that her soul was conflicted about doing so, but you begged for your life. You begged to survive so you could fight for the salvation of your soul. We all agreed that your soul must be saved, and we encouraged Suzette to bite you," Henrietta says.

"This is a nightmare," Victor says.

Suzette could see horror and disgust in his eyes.

Victor ignores their eyes. The smell of rotting flesh commingling with embalming fluid is too much for Victor's shocked and confused mind. He walks out of the airless room without excusing himself.

Suzette dissolved into bloody tears.

"Give him time to process what just happened," Maximus says to the inconsolable Suzette.

"He is well hydrated. He can go for a couple of days without needing blood. He will have plenty of time to reflect and remember that he begged for you to save him," Henrietta says to Suzette.

"Yes, he begged to be saved. Even in his desperate state, I am sure, he expected salvation to be granted by holy water and science—not in such a monstrous manner. I lost him," Suzette says between sobs.

"He will come around. More than ever, he needs us," Ivan assures Suzette.

The receding afternoon sun irritates his skin as he briskly walks home. Visions of the devil's seabed, Goldendeath, and the indescribable pain from the demon vampire dog torment his mind and body.

Once in his room at the Maison de Ville, he sits down in the dark with a bottle of rum and drinks and drinks until he passes out. The streams of sunlight that filter in from the huge windows soon assault him, forcing him awake. Not letting go of the rum in his hand, he jumps up and presses himself into the corner of two walls next to the door. His instinctual response to the sun horrifies him. He downs rum as the images from the hellish day before terrorize him. He curses the day he arrived in New Orleans. He fled California with a broken heart. He will now return to California without a soul.

His inner battle is demoralizing. He recognizes that he momentarily escaped the devil, but still he lost his soul. Losing his soul is hell in itself. The word *salvation* dominates his thoughts. His soul is cocooned in a monster body among the living, not burning in the lake of fire. He tells himself he must fight for the salvation of his soul. A fight that must be fought away from New Orleans and that community of monsters that masquerade themselves as kinder spirits. Anger boils in him. He is angry for being so blinded by the pain of unrequited love to not see the markings of the monsters that encircle him with unspoken truths and seduction. He feels he must save his soul from its monstrous existence and the gates of hell. His thoughts turn to Suzette and Ivan. Conflict and anger consume him. He understands that secrecy is paramount for their existence. Their secrecy damned him. His forsaken soul wrestles to find where to put the blame. He thinks of Suzette. Out of love, she used the only power she had to claw him back from the depths of hell. Victor painfully understands that one cannot rule over one's heart. That Suzette's need to have him close to her resulted in her hiding her monstrous side. Victor does not know how to feel. His thoughts go to his family, and he worries about the horror they will suffer when they learn that while away to heal a broken heart, he lost his soul to darkness.

The bottle of rum in his hand is not yet empty. He slowly drinks to get the edge off. He feels his senses sharpening up as he learns to navigate his new reality, and he hopes his senses will guard him from the gates of hell. With that thought, he instinctually feels a familiar energy on the other side of the door. He pulls his attention away from the door and back to his bottle of rum.

"Let me in, Victor."

"Leave me alone with my thoughts," Victor pleads.

"That is what I am afraid of, leaving you to your thoughts."

Victor can hear life stirring outside his windows. He looks out, and like a promise, the sun is bright. The glistening of the morning dew on the leaves of the trees assaults his eyes. The energetic chirping of birds as they fly away from the shadows and into the light mocks his soul. The normalcy of the world continues, but his sense normalcy will now be challenged day in, day out.

"I have something to confess."

The door swings open and hits the wall next to him. Henrietta glides in, wearing a heavy cloak that covers her head to protect her from the morning sun and muffles the sounds of birds singing.

"That you are a vampire?" Victor snarls with a mocking tone.

"Do not be afraid to use your gifts," Henrietta instructs as she lifts her hands and claps the heavy curtains shut. She uncovers her head and states, "It is not an illusion, but true magic."

"Dark magic," Victor bellows.

"I was the one who demanded that you be saved so that you can fight for your soul. From your desperate words and suffering, I assumed that you would rather be confined to this world and not be spirited away to a darkness you will not be able to escape," Henrietta warmly explains.

"Suzette..." Victor begins.

"Suzette was tortured. It was life or death. Salvation or damnation. Light or darkness. Condemning you in life or letting you pass on to your hellish prison. Exposing herself as a monster to the man she loves. It was the hardest choice in her existence. Above all, her concern was for your soul. We all are worried about your soul."

"How does damning me save my soul?" Victor implores.

"Your damned soul, as you put it, will buy you time to fight. You are a rarity in our community. You begged for life to save your soul. You did not beg for immortality because you were seduced by darkness. There must be a way for you to one day pass in peace and rest in peace. But dying on that slab, with the gates of hell opened for you, was not the answer."

Victor walks out of his corner and stands in front of her. His hypnotic gray eyes study her. And then he protests, "If you all were honest with me, I would not have been in this predicament. I am most surprised by Ivan. I misjudged him."

"Ivan did not know that Goldendeath is the devil's servant and collector of souls. Have you forgotten? It was Ivan who fought off the demon dogs. Ivan's distress call helped you get transported to Suzette's plantation. Ivan did not know. Nobody knew. It would not serve Goldendeath for word to get out. Such is the torment that Goldendeath, who was once viewed as the devil himself, tries to escape hell one soul at a time."

"Let's not pretend that my soul has any value for you. You fought for my damnation so that I am the object of Suzette's affection, not Ivan."

"True. But, I have also grown to hold you in high esteem. To see you suffering and on the cusp of losing your soul, through no fault of your own, mortified and worried me. You need a tool to fight, and the only tool was immortality."

"God. Why did I not call out to God? It was Jesus who saved us from the demon dogs. Why did not I call out to God?" Victor exclaims.

"The demons clouded your brain with pain and hallucinations. In your moments of lucidity, your energy went to us in the room. And you begged to be saved so you could fight for your soul."

Henrietta watches as Victor paces the room. The memories of his torment bombard him as he searches for answers. After a couple of minutes, Victor stops pacing and reasons, "Since the devil did not take me when I was on that slab, who can say he still has a right to me? Goldendeath lost. My soul is not in hell."

"But we do not know that for sure. What is certain is that there is a battle between good and evil, and I can bet you the devil does not like to lose. The devil will not walk away from the battle to own your soul," Henrietta says.

The heaviness in the room intensifies as Victor trembles with rage and regret. Henrietta steps back, away from him.

"Goldendeath did not lose. The devil did not lose. My soul is as condemned today as it would have been had I died on that slab. I am now a monster. For now, I have been granted a stay, but in time, my sentence in hell will commence," Victor thunders.

A knock on the door, which is marked with a "Do Not Disturb" sign, breaks through the anguish in the room.

"Urgent message for Señor Montenegro," a young man's voice rings out.

A note is pushed through the bottom crack of the door. Victor picks up the note.

His mother is ill.

"I need to depart to California," Victor announces.

Henrietta trembles with anxiety as she desperately asks, "What about Suzette?"

"As the sun rose this morning, my feelings for her darkened. I understand that out of desperation and of me begging for salvation she used darkness to save me, for the time being, from hell. But I do not know if I can forget that she lied to me," Victor says.

Henrietta's pleading eyes fail to move Victor. Looking at her with contempt, he says, "You too deceived me. In your plight to keep Ivan's affections, you failed to warn me that I was seduced by a monster."

"In the name of love," Henrietta declares.

Victor walks to his wardrobe, opens it, and he begins to move his clothes from the wardrobe to the trunk next to it.

"It will destroy Suzette if you leave without talking to her!"

"She is indestructible," Victor says.

Victor turns to look at Henrietta, and he says, "Ivan will not let harm come to her. She is in good hands. Ivan is a good man. Unlike you and Suzette, he struggles with his darkness. Looking back, it all makes sense, his peace with death and his desire for death."

"Suzette means nothing to you?" Henrietta asks.

"I am not sure what I feel now. I need to sort out my feelings. I need to come to terms with…"

"With the new you," Henrietta interjects.

Victor stops his packing and turns to look at Henrietta, dismay clouding over his gray eyes.

"I must find a way to go back to my old self. Please leave, Henrietta. I need to depart as soon as possible," Victor demands.

"Would you like to leave word for Suzette?" Henrietta requests.

"Words fail me. Right now, I am not in the position to think about anyone else but my mother."

MONTENEGRO BOOK TWO: DARK SERENADE

His arrival home is too late. Victor arrives at the Montenegro train station at the moment his mother exhales her last breath. On the busy platform, Victor freezes from the arresting feeling that his mother has passed. By all accounts, it is a normal night. The trains are on time. Passengers continue with their routines. The steam from the trains filters through the outline of the trees. A normal evening in every sense to everyone but Victor. Victor feels betrayed and cruelly punished. Within a matter of days, he plunged into the devil's seabed and escaped hell by turning into a monster. He lost his mother without saying good-bye. A chain of events brought on by his desperation to run away from a broken heart. If he had remained in California, he would have continued with his normal life, and perhaps his mother would still be alive, or at the very least he would have been at her side as she departed from this world. He looks around, and he wishes his life was normal, like the lives of those who hurry around him. Living in darkness while fighting for his soul within a loveless existence is now his new normal.

As he hears the familiar sounds of the coach's horses galloping through the cobbled streets of his familial city, Montenegro, Victor, grieving the loss of his mother, looks down at his handkerchief and discovers, to his horror, that he has shed blood tears. He composes himself. No one can ever see him shed a blood tear. As the son of a stoic governor who survived an attempt on his life by a rival politician, no one will question Victor's lack of outward emotion. Victor focuses on his blessings. He is grateful that he is not in hell, that his mother did not die mourning his death, and, most importantly, that his mother will never learn that, while in New Orleans, he became a monster.

His mother's sister and his younger sister meet Victor at the entrance of the foyer, their ashen faces streaked with tears. Every mirror in the estate is draped with a dark cloth. His older brother, who is the mayor of Montenegro, is not home to greet Victor because of his civic duties. "Her last word was your name," his grieving aunt says.

His mother succumbed to the very disease she built a hospital to battle: consumption.

"We just could not keep her from the hospital and away from the dying patients," his grieving sister regrets.

"It was her mission to help the sick, and she knew the risks. Have peace in knowing that our beloved late mother is now reunited with our late father. May they both rest in peace," Victor says.

The dark circular glasses that he wore on the rainy day of his mother's public funeral have become a daily accessory. His family, as well as the townspeople, surmise that Victor's dark glasses are his perpetual way of mourning his mother while shielding the sadness in the town's most talked about gray eyes. His glasses are for mourning his mother, but they also serve to shield his eyes from the sun. Victor's family, still in mourning, does not protest, nor does his staff question, Victor's orders to remove all the mirrors from the estate, which will prevent anyone from discovering that the mirrors will not reflect his image. The mirrors that remain are in the private chambers of his aunt, sister, and brother. It torments Victor that while he is mourning his mother's death, he is also mourning his lost soul. He fears that because his soul is claimed by the devil and his body claimed by darkness, his family will be cursed and suffer destruction in his shadow. It is a daily battle to fight his mind and not view himself as a walking corpse and to refuse to believe that his heart is a half dead. He feels forsaken and without mercy, but it will not stop him from fighting for salvation. His desperation, while asleep or awake, to discover a way to rescue his soul robs him of the everyday joys of life. Weeks after his mother's death, the sightings of Victor during the day are so few and far between that the citizens of Montenegro fear that Victor's mother's death has transformed the gregarious illusionist into an elusive public servant. Victor turns a deaf ear on what is said about him, as he finds comfort that the death of his mother has spared her from living with the pain of learning that her son is a monster whose soul is consigned to the devil.

Victor, over the course of two months, and with finesse, accustoms his family, friends, associates, and staff to his preference for night over day. Victor slowly accustoms the humans around him to his heightened magical prowess. His illusions, enhanced by his monstrosity, become the talk of the town. In the plazas, in the early evening hours, Victor performs magic tricks for the children. The public gets fired up by his amazing tricks, but the profound emptiness in his unshielded eyes is not lost on most of the spectators. To explain the emptiness in his eyes, a rumor spreads that while Victor was in New Orleans, a dark voodoo priestess gave him a charm to enhance his illusions in exchange for his soul—a pact that he now regrets and that causes him to wander the night, bemoaning selling his soul.

Three months after arriving in California, Victor receives a letter from Suzette. Victor holds the unopened letter in his hand, and he can feel her heartfelt condolences for the loss of his mother, her anguish to know his thoughts about her. Her conflict of whether she did what was right on the day his soul was promised to the devil. Her longing for him with a broken heart. The emotions rising from the unopened letter are too much for his conflicted soul to bear, let alone letting her words further describe her torment. Victor feels for Suzette, but his resentment about her hiding her darkness from him is more powerful than his will. He is not ready to communicate with her, not while he is still mourning the loss of his mother and his damnation.

Suzette's broken heart forces him to think about his heartbreak over Clara. His heartache over the ending of his engagement to Clara is even more painful with the realization that it was unrequited love that broke them up, and now his cruel fate will be unrequited love. Despite his heartache and the constant torment that his final destination will be the lake of fire, he manages to mask his darkness while hiding behind his magic. However, with each day that passes, it is becoming more challenging to deceive his older brother. His brother keeps an attentive eye on Victor, and when his brother is not attending to his duties as mayor, he takes the opportunity to question and probe Victor, pointing out on several occasions that outside of his passion and talent for magic, he is not the same man. That the void and sadness he sees in Victor's eyes go beyond a son who lost his mother and a man who lost his fiancée.

Victor does not want to burden his brother with his dark secret. He needs to protect his family and the family name. Victor fears that if it gets out that he is a vampire, the townspeople will lynch his family. Thus, when the post for an ambassador to Mexico opens, Victor takes the job and flees to Mexico, where he can hide his darkness from his family and community.

In the courtyard of his diplomatic home, underneath a canopy of stars, with a melodic water fountain that cools the air, scented by the evening flowers, Victor escapes darkness in the beauty of serenity. Sitting on the stone bench with a glass of brandy, he lets the calming silence drown out his thoughts.

"Silence is the most feared dagger to the heart."

Victor looks at the shadow across the courtyard. His serenity shatters as conflict crashes down on him.

He removes his hat, and then he demands, "How did you find me?"

"It is a gift from the darkness."

Victor stands up and looks toward the closed gates at the back of the property.

"I can appreciate you needing to run away from darkness, but I implore you, do not walk away from me," Suzette begs as she glides across the courtyard to stand next to him.

Victor looks down at her eyes, marked with sorrow. Suzette wraps her arms around his neck and holds him close to her, and she says, "I am very sorry about your mother."

Victor grips his hat tight, and with his other free hand, he presses his open palm into her back and then pulls away. Suzette slowly lowers her rejected arms.

"Thank you, but you could have mailed your condolences," Victor says.

"So that you would leave it unopened and unread, like my last letter?" Suzette says.

The pain in her voice echoes through him.

"Forgive me. I am a lost soul, and I do not know how to feel," Victor says.

"I love you. I will always love you," Suzette declares.

"For eternity," Victor says, defeated.

"Yes, an eternity. We have an eternity. An eternity to rescue your soul. An eternity in a world where love still resides. An eternity with beautiful nights like tonight. An eternity," Suzette encourages.

"I realize that I begged you to save my life for the mercy of my soul. Given the circumstances, it was the only path. But it was the path I was put on by your willful deceit. Had I known that you are a mistress of darkness, I would have not been intimate with you," Victor says.

He stands up and looks at the brilliant moon. Suzette eyes, clouded by blood, also look up to the moon.

"I sought refuge from my heartache in your arms, hoping that I would fall in love with you. I feared that my heart was too broken to love again, but in reality, it had nothing to do with my broken heart," Victor pauses, looks at Suzette, and then continues, "It was not my broken heart that prevented me from loving you. It was your damned heart."

Suzette leans toward him and says, "There is a part of you that feels that you could have loved me."

"I now understand why I can never love you."

"Our damned hearts are still capable of affection, warmth, and desire," Suzette says.

"My broken heart was more whole than my condemned heart," Victor laments as he stares into the darkness behind her.

"I pray that you forgive me. You are my true love, and I was afraid to lose you if you knew the truth. I was hoping that, with time, you would learn the truth about me, but I never dreamed it would be in the clutches of the devil."

"In the clutches of the devil—befitting, don't you agree? Forgive me, my dear, if I do not lavish you with my attention. My focus now is how I am going to tell my family that I am damned and that my soul is in danger. I need to figure how I can return to my ancestral home without my community wanting me destroyed."

Suzette sits down on an ornate wooden bench. The moon, hidden by a lush tree, leaves her in total darkness as blood tears trail down her pale face.

Victor puts back on his hat and stands over her. He informs Suzette, "On the day I was summoned home, Henrietta came to see me. She explained that she implored you to save my life. That although you were conflicted, you did so out of love and for the sake of my soul. I understand that a heart in love has no reason. I cannot dwell on what cannot be undone. I still have life to fight for my soul and to care for my family. I owe it to my grandfather to be a good steward to the citizens of Montenegro."

"You need our vampire community as much as we need you. There is strength in numbers," Suzette says.

"What monster did this to you?" Victor demands.

"It was not a monster. It was Ivan."

Victor's incredulous eyes study her, and he says, "Ivan? Ivan is one of the most upstanding gentlemen I've had the privilege of meeting."

"He thinks highly of you as well. And he laments what happened to you. He saved you from the diabolic teeth of the demon dog that could have kept you with its teeth in the devil's seabed until your slow and agonizing death, tormented by demons, delivered your soul to the devil." Suzette pauses to compose herself, and with a wavering voice, she informs Victor, "I am not a victim. I begged Ivan to…"

"To damn you? For the love of God, why?"

"The real monster is death. I did not want to live fearing death."

"Death is not a monster. Damnation is the monster."

"Forgive me," Suzette implores.

Victor sits down next to Suzette. He raises his open palm to her. Suzette rests her shaking hand on his palm, and Victor kisses it.

"I fear death now too because I know that after death, I will have to face damnation. Is there anything else that you are keeping from me?"

"I consort with werewolves and hire witches," Suzette says.

"In my previous life, so to speak, that would scandalize me, but now it seems normal."

"What are your plans? You will be the talk of the town as the citizens age, but you do not," Suzette warns.

Victor stares at the fountain that is loudly cascading water over two ornate tiered bowls.

"I am told that this fountain is over two hundred years old. People are more intrigued by its age than its soothing functionality. I can remain functional for centuries, but people will not focus on my functionality. They will be intrigued as to why I am not aging."

"This is why mortals can never know your true age. Good or evil monster, you are still a monster. In order to live on, for as long as the earth is whole, you will have to feign deaths. You will need to reinvent yourself, be born again and again," Suzette advises.

Victor looks at Suzette, and then he utters, "You are the orphan who traveled to New Orleans as casket girl."

"Precisely. And throughout my whole existence, I practiced medicine and managed my plantation. The world understands that the ancestors of Suzette Savarit all share the passion for medicine and the posterity of the plantation. You do not need quit your passions."

"I pray that my siblings will be accepting of my fate and supportive in my plight to save my soul. The city of Montenegro is a small one, and I am afraid that when they learn I am monster, they will not only take my life but the lives of my family," Victor says, worried.

"No one outside of your family needs to learn that you are a vampire. Use your post and time here in Mexico to reinvent a new identity. After a few decades, return to Montenegro as the spitting-image son, Victor Montenegro, of the late Victor Montenegro. And, as the son, you inherited his famous gray eyes and canny magical prowess," Suzette advises.

Victor looks at the water in the fountain and says, "I must admit that having to deal with my new normal has been an emotional hell. What has helped me deal with it is my passion for magic, albeit enhanced by darkness. I will not fool myself. There is no magic in this world that can save my soul from the clutches of the devil. I will pray for intervention and do my best to earn my salvation."

"I am here for you. I always will be here for you, come what may. I deeply regret your hell on earth, but I find immense peace that you are not suffering in the lake of fire."

"How long is your stay?" Victor asks.

"I would like to stay for a few weeks. I want to behold the sunsets over the beautiful beaches and the colonial cities you talked about. If you will have me," Suzette pleads.

"I have conflicted feelings for you. Meeting you has drastically changed my life and my soul's journey. I realize now that your life was never in danger the night we met. I was lost and lonely and sought refuge in the feelings you developed for me. Had I known you are a mistress of darkness, I would not have pursued you intimately. If I could find a way to go back in time, I would have pulled you over the opera balcony and then immediately returned to my normal life in California. But there is no going back, and I have to accept things as they are. I cannot fight for my soul if I live in denial."

A breeze pushes through the trees hovering over them, and leaves rain down on them. Tears escape Suzette eyes as she looks down to brush the dead leaves from her lap with her shaky hands. She then looks up at Victor with pleading red eyes, and before she has a chance to speak Victor continues, "I care about you, Suzette. I know that you are not an evil person at heart. The pain in your life and the fear of death steered you into a dark existence. I am blessed that I belong to a tight-knit family, but they will struggle with my darkness, let alone understanding my new reality. I need you, and I need the vampire community."

"I will forever love you. There is no light or darkness that has the power to kill my love for you. I need to be in your life. I feel I have the responsibility to give you the support and guidance that only a vampire can."

"You will need to forgive me. Superficial intimacy is just a reminder that I am a monster. I still struggle with knowing that mutual love is forbidden. The devil stealing my whole heart has robbed my desire for intimacy."

"Give it time, and you will see that your desire will once again burn. In time, you will be reminded that intimacy is what still connects us to the human race."

"I feel you will love the charm of the colonial cities," Victor says, pressing the back of her hand against his heart.

Wolf Tower

"I do not hold any resentment toward you. I have respect for you and appreciate you saving me from the clutches of that damned demon dog. I hope that, in time, I can repay you," Victor says as he and Ivan share a bottle of rum and pints of foreign werewolf blood.

"Well, I am here to collect. I want the *Ana Luisa*'s treasure, and especially the most coveted treasure of all her ships—the *San Esteban*."

"It is not just the treasure that you desire but battling Goldendeath," Victor says.

Ivan looks at Victor. Victor's gray skin and fangs give him conflicted stomach pangs.

"I do not have the words to express my deep lament that your life and your soul's journey have been altered, altered by my capricious quest for the *Ana Luisa*," Ivan expresses.

"Do not beat yourself up, brother. I went along willingly and just as hungry for the *Ana Luisa*. You had no idea that we would wind up in the devil's seabed. You had no idea that the *Ana Luisa* is Goldendeath's soul-devouring maiden. If it were not for you, I would be dead and suffering the torments in the lake of fire," Victor says as he warmly pats Ivan on his shoulder.

"You are right. It angers me that Goldendeath uses the *Ana Luisa* to seduce treasure hunters so he can cash in on their souls to escape the hell that he richly deserves. However, our immortality cannot afford him escape. Goldendeath has no use for us."

"I am sure the devil made him pay because I escaped with my life and, more importantly, with my soul. Goldendeath will gladly receive us for the opportunity to avenge us for making a mockery of him in the eyes of the devil."

Victor smiles at the delicious irony. The idea of facing off with Goldendeath and his damned minions is exciting. But his focus right now is reinventing himself so that he can go home to his family and his community.

"I am glad that we met here at Wolf Tower. My sudden departure from New Orleans and facing my demons did not allow for me to thank you."

"I am sorry about your mother," Ivan says.

"Thank you. I am comforted that she passed without becoming aware that her beloved son is a monster. She left to a better world, and I hope she rests in peace without any knowledge of my hellish predicament," Victor prays.

Victor looks around; Wolf Tower is bustling with immortal creatures. It still unnerves him to be around so much darkness.

"I need another quarter of a century or so before I will be ready to follow you into the devil's seabed. We have time. The *Ana Luisa's* treasure and those of her ships will not be raised from hell," Victor assures him.

"Fair. It took me a half of century to deal with my darkness. A quarter of a century is but a blink of an eye in eternity. What are your plans for the next twenty-five years?" Ivan asks him.

"My post as the ambassador to Mexico for the last twenty-five years has kept the townspeople in Montenegro and my family in the dark about my vampirism. I fear that those around me in Mexico will start to question why I have not aged. I distract people's inquisitive eyes with my magical prowess, but that smoke screen cannot protect me for much longer. I was able to wrangle into being the ambassador for Spain. I will be among people whom I have never met, and without having to fear suspicion, I will be able to breathe again."

Pain strikes Ivan's heart. He reaches for the rum as he remembers Suzette sharing her plan with him about buying a home in Spain for seasonal trips that will benefit her sugar trade. Ivan now realizes that her home in Spain is not so much about sugar but to be near Victor.

"My hatred for darkness at times makes me want to be alone so I can wallow in pity. However, the overwhelming alienation from hiding my monstrosity and living through the deaths of those around me makes me crave company. The best company comes from fellow suffers of the darkness," Victor admits.

Ivan solemnly nods.

Victor pours more rum into Ivan's glass and refills his, and then he confesses, "I do not want to feed my darkness with hate, rancor, and suspicion. I will reserve those feelings for the devil—the true actor of my darkness. I cannot phantom the agony that all of you had to deal with during my delirium on that forsaken day of my transformation. The lot of you did what you all deemed would be the best route to save my soul, and for that, I am eternally grateful. While I have not returned to New Orleans, I have been visited regularly by Suzette in Mexico."

Ivan weakly smiles as he drinks more rum.

"For a creature of darkness, Suzette has the patience of a saint. I am aware that she still loves me, and we are all aware that I am not in love with her. I regret the number of times I have hurt her by denying her wish to put me in the Amare trance. In my darkness and despair, there is no room for artificial love. Suzette provides the support I need and companionship in my estate away from the sun, but being intimate with her is like making love not to her but to darkness. I keep the company of other women, women whose hearts are whole."

Ivan nods sympathetically, but he refrains from answering. He is in love with Suzette, and he appreciates Victor's friendship. Ivan does not want to meddle with them, as much as he does not want Victor to meddle in his relationship with Suzette.

"What is your plan for the next twenty-five years?" Ivan asks.

"The next twenty-five years will be my road back home from Spain. My body has not aged a day; I do not look a day past thirty years old. I cannot visit home now. I will need to prepare my family from afar for the shock they will suffer when they set eyes on me again. Suzette advised that I reinvent myself. Aside from my illusions, I am not an actor, and it will be a challenge to feign that I am someone else. Magic is the only constant in my life. I cannot phantom not performing illusions; being void of magic in my life will destroy my spirit," Victor says in a sad tone.

"You will not have to give up your gift of illusion, brother," Ivan says confidently.

"How so?" Victor eagerly asks.

"Suzette has not given up medicine. I have not given up treasure hunting. We all kept our passions, and so can you. Return to your beloved Montenegro as the son of the late Victor Montenegro, who died from cholera. You not only inherited his gray eyes and an uncanny resemblance to him but also his passion for illusions and his cache of magical tricks. While your family will welcome the true Victor Montenegro home, the citizens of Montenegro will welcome his son," Ivan recommends.

For the first time since that infamous day when he escaped the devil's seabed, Victor smiles with happiness. The darkness will not completely engulf his image; he will hold on to what really defines passion for him: his mastery of illusions.

The Envelope

In a series of letters home, Victor methodically and delicately describes what happened to him when he was in New Orleans. In the letters to his older brother Ernesto and younger sister Sofia, he asks for mercy, support, and love as he lives with a darkness he did not willingly choose. His sister's letters arrive dotted with her tears, filled with love, full of questions and fears. The silence from his older brother is deafening and painful. For years, he continues to receive letters from his sister, still filled with love, support, and news from home and about the town of Montenegro. Her most recent letter brings the sad news that his beloved aunt, his mother's sister, passed in her sleep. Sofia writes that Victor should mourn with the comfort that their aunt died not knowing about his darkness and that she will continue to intervene on his behalf with their older brother.

On the day that marks twenty-five years in Spain, an envelope arrives from his older brother. Victor eagerly opens the envelope. In the envelope, there is not a long-awaited letter but the official death certificate of Victor Montenegro, with cholera listed as the cause of death. Victor's heart drops, and unspeakable sadness buries him. As he folds his death certificate, he notices that it has attachments. The first attachment is the official birth certificate of Victor Montenegro, son of Victor Montenegro and Lisa Montenegro.

The last attachment is the official, albeit forged, death certificate of Lisa Montenegro, the fictitious mother of the reinvented Victor Montenegro. Ernesto, Victor's older brother, is the mayor of Montenegro, and Victor knows that obtaining the fraudulent documents would require at most a few of days, but Ernesto waited years. Victor is grateful that his brother is now being supportive, but it still hurts that it took his brother twenty-five years—twenty-five years of him pleading; twenty-five years of tears and pleading from his younger sister. Victor immediately departs for his beloved Montenegro, California.

City of Montenegro, 1903

Victor Montenegro's homecoming is emotional and jarring to his soul. His siblings' faces are marked with time. His brother's once dark raven hair is now as white as the snow of his long European winters. Through walls of tears, Sofia studies the ageless Victor, and then she blankets his face with kisses. His nephew and nieces, now young adults, will need to remember to treat their uncle as their young cousin while in public. To his surprise and relief, his brother receives him with a hug and says, "Forgive me…"

"I am just grateful to be with my family and back in my beloved city," Victor says with forgiveness in his eyes.

Soon after he arrives, there is a public homecoming for Victor, and he is formally introduced to the citizens of Montenegro as Victor Montenegro, the only living heir of the much-beloved and still mourned late master illusionist Victor Montenegro Senior. After the homecoming, his sister attends evening mass, as she has been doing for the past twenty-five years, to pray for Victor's soul. Ernesto, with a stoic face, instructs Victor to learn as much as he can about the current civics of Montenegro because, in time, he will need to run for mayor and continue to be the living steward of their familial city. Victor's nephew encourages him to enchant their friends with his magical prowess. And soon the town catches on that the young Victor Montenegro is blessed with the art of illusion of his supposed late father. Victor eagerly takes to the stage, grateful that the magician in him does not need to hide.

Julieta Maria Avila

With his hat pulled down closer to his face, his collar raised, and carrying a walking stick, Victor navigates through the crowd on his way back home from a successful twilight hunt for rodents for him to feed on.

Haunted by the isolation of his monstrosity, Victor keeps his gray eyes focused on the cobblestone streets as he slowly makes his way back to his estate. Victor spots a couple of politicians; not wishing to be recognized, Victor cuts into an alley that ushers him into a public square that the elite will only traverse when they lose their way. As he crosses the public square, his thoughts of despair are interrupted by a female voice ringing out a beautiful aria. Victor stops and looks toward the gathering of people. Standing next to a modest fountain is a woman singing. Next to her stands a young boy. The people around the public square are mesmerized by her beautiful singing. The windows on the buildings that circle the public square are open, and people lean from them to hear her sing.

Victor, unrecognized, makes his way to the front of the crowd. The woman sings her song as if she were the only soul standing in the public square; her passionate singing moves everyone into an awed silence. Her caramel eyes look at no one. Her chocolate hair cascades over her well-worn cloak. Despite her modest clothing, her singing speaks of a rich background in music.

The crowd grows and moves in closer toward her with each note she sings. Without music to accompany her, her voice passionately echoes through the public square. The profoundness in her passion, her spirit, and the depth in her eyes enthrall Victor. Victor is not the only man enchanted by the passionate songstress. Standing to the far left of Victor is a man who ventured into the public square in the hopes of hearing the songstress—Julieta Maria Avila—sing. His dark cloak and hat conceal him. He is a publicly known person who enjoys roaming the streets without being recognized. He stands still to listen to Julieta sing. And, like Julieta, he is also very passionate about the art of music. His name is Carlo Fini, and he is an internationally known and lauded gifted violinist. Carlo Fini's music brings audiences to complete silence as they live every note he plays. By Fini's attire and posture, Victor can tell he is a man of substance, but he fails to recognize him. Carlo Fini can feel Victor's discreet eyes trying to read him. Carlo, without lifting his head from the shadow of his tall hat, slightly turns toward Victor, and Victor can read on his face that he is enchanted with the songstress.

The thunderous applause gives Julieta the courage to smile as the young boy walks around the crowd with his cap in hand to collect donations from the moved crowd. Victor pulls out three gold coins and places them in the boy's small hand. The overjoyed boy's eyes are met by Victor's famous gray eyes, and Victor pleads anonymity with a wink of his eye. The young boy smiles and continues his collection.

Victor observes as Carlo walks up to Julieta. Carlo tips his hat and gallantly bows, kisses her hand, quickly puts his hat back on, and then says, "I am here to bask in your light and hear your gifted voice." Victor sees recognition of Carlo in Julieta's eyes. Victor walks away from the public square with Julieta's passionate song still ringing in his ears and the determination to learn everything he can about the captivating songstress.

Carlo Fini

Carlo's father possesses a passion for music, but he lacks talent. His father numbs his rancor for his dead musical career by drinking. When Carlo first picked up a violin at age five, his father recognized that Carlo had the talent that was not bestowed on him. Since then, with brute force, his father has pushed Carlo to live the life he dreamed of achieving, which is world domination through music. Being the recipient of praise for his son's talent encourages Carlo's father to demand perfection from Carlo's violin. As the venues and crowds for Carlo's performances grow, his father's ambitiousness grows. In his angry tongue lashings, Carlo's father accuses him of being ungrateful; his father also accuses Carlo of intentionally not realizing his full potential as a violinist to spite him. His father's overbearing demands exhaust Carlo, but they do not deplete his passion for music. Carlo is relieved, for his father's sake, that his abuse has not killed the talent he was born with. However, it pains him to see his ill mother suffer as she witnesses the emotional and mental attacks rained down on him because of his father's insatiable hunger for international success.

To afford his mother some peace from the storm between him and his father, Carlo takes refuge in a local tavern. He sits close to the wall at a table hidden in the shadows. Drinking his third beer, he wishes for the day when he can enjoy playing for an audience without having to dread facing his father at the end of the show. With every performance, his father becomes more critical and insufferable. He thinks of his mother, who continues to fight death so as to not leave him alone with his brute of a father. Similarly, Carlo refuses to leave his ill mother alone with his father. Secretly, he wishes the grace of death would take his mother away from her suffering. Carlo prays for long life for his father so that he will live to see him attain the fame that his father hungers for unmercifully, at which point he plans to ceremonially shun him.

"Music is a moral law. It gives soul to the universe, wings to the mind, flight to the imagination, a charm to sadness, gaiety and life to everything; it is the essence of order and lends to all that is good, just, and beautiful," says a dapperly dressed man as he sits down across from Carlo.

"Plato," Carlo says.

"Indeed. Do you agree with Plato?" the man asks.

"Yes, I do," Carlo answers.

"Of course you do, Señor Carlo Fini."

Carlo studies the well-dressed man with dark eyes, and then he asks, "And you are?"

The man extends his hand across the table, and as Carlo shakes his gloved hand, the man introduces himself as Steve Hamlin.

"I do not believe we ever met, Mr. Hamlin," Carlo says.

"I've watched your career over the years. You have unsung talent," Steve says.

The air between them is charged; Carlo pulls back against his seat. The intensity in Steve's eyes unnerves him. Carlo turns away from the table and calls out to the waitress and asks for more beer. Carlo turns back around, and he is greeted with a refilled beer. Carlo looks to see if the other waitress is close by, but the two waitresses are across the tavern, attending to other customers. Carlo looks at

Steve. Steve gives him an eerie smile, then he says, "The beer is on me, Mr. Fini."

"Thank you. How did you get the glass filled?" Carlo asks.

"Impressed? You will be more impressed with what can be done with your career," Steve says.

"I am not interested in working with an illusionist," Carlo says.

"I am not an illusionist," Steve says as he makes the beer in the glass boil.

"Well, I will need another…"

Another beer appears in front of Carlo.

"Very impressive. You've found your calling, Mr. Hamlin. But I am not your audience," Carlo says with a dismissive hand.

"I wish for you to meet the kingmaker," Steve announces.

Carlo can feel his skin crawl and, in the depths of him, the desire to flee.

"You are still here," Steve says with a laugh, and then he says, "I am not going to speak through smoke and mirrors, but we do need privacy."

The noise in the tavern halts, and every living creature is frozen in time. The spirits that were being poured at the bar freeze in midair.

Carlo tightens his fist. Steve removes his hat and lets it fall on top of the table. Carlo feels as though he is trapped in a photograph.

"Now that I have your audience, in the beginning of time, there was an angel. An angel with a gift for music. In fact, he was blessed by God as his chief musician of the universe. Over the centuries, the chief has not relinquished his role as chief or his passion for music. Allow me to introduce you to my boss." Steve stands up, and as he glides back, he announces, "The great Satan."

A towering figure materializes in front of Carlo. The beast is not as he would have imagined him. Despite his eight-foot stature, he is dressed like a presentable gentleman. Satan's eyes are lakes of fire that look at Carlo.

The debilitating fear storming through Carlo impairs him from remembering a prayer to dispatch the fallen angel.

"Relax, Mr. Fini. I come as a friend," Satan says as he removes his hat and sits down across from Carlo.

"I'm a great fan of your music. You are a gifted violinist who should be applauded throughout the world. Your father, despite his hunger for world fame, lacks the ability to market you. I offer you the entire world as your stage. I will give you the ability to write music that will place you among history's greatest composers. I will give you the stamina to play without exhaustion. You will be written into history as one of the greatest violinists known to man," Satan seduces.

"In exchange for what?" Carlo says in a terrified whisper.

"Your adoration…"

"You do not seek the adoration of this modest soul," Carlo retorts.

"You are deeply mistaken. I seek the adoration of every living soul."

Carlo shifts in his seat, and then he glides his hand along the uneven tabletop; he can feel the heads of the nails. The terror has not subsided, but curiosity rises in him. He is not overly religious, but he understands that Satan is the chief of lies.

"I am not lying," Satan says.

"You demand more than adoration," Carlo counters.

"When your body fails you, I want you and your music in my realm for the posterity of future musicians' souls," Satan says.

"You want my soul condemned to hell," Carlo argues.

"Yes, I want your soul and every other soul on this planet. I am no different than God. He too wants your soul, but he is not offering you anything in return. I have the power to make your life on earth like heaven in exchange for your soul."

Satan unfurls a parchment with Carlo's name in bold at the top and places it on the table. Carlo thinks about his insufferable father and his suffering mother. He thinks about how his life would be worthless without music. Throughout his life, he has interpreted others' music. The idea of musicians giving life to his music is exhilarating. His burning desire to silence his father's criticism with fame is undeniable.

Satan breaks into his thoughts and adds, "Fame will free you from all sacrifices."

Carlo thinks about his perpetual pursuit of fame, for which he has sacrificed living life and pursuing love.

"With fame, you will have the power of allurement and hence the desire of women."

Carlo's thoughts go to Julieta, and his heart swells.

"I will agree to sign if you agree to grant me three wishes when I request them," Carlo demands.

Satan's guttural laugh thunders in the stillness of the tavern. Satan's grotesque claws wave over the contract, and Carlo watches as his three wishes are written in blood.

Satan plucks a quill from the air and stabs Carlo's heart with the quill. Satan then pulls the quill out of his heart. He hands the quill, dripping with his blood, to Carlo, then Satan says, "Once you sign, you will be Carlo Fini, world-renowned violinist, courted by women, the envy of musicians, and courted by royals."

Carlo signs the contract, and his world is transformed. The second he dots the last *i* on his name, he is transported to the front of his modest home, which is now a museum to the living legend Carlo Fini. Instinctively, he finds his way home—a mansion standing in one of the finest plazas in Montenegro. He enters his grand home to find his mother in better health. His banished father, accompanied by rum and his pride for his illustrious son, is sequestered in an apartment across town that is owned by Carlo.

On the evening after his deal with the devil, in a quaint

passageway to the main plaza, Carlo and Victor cross paths. Lifting their hats, they acknowledge each other and then part ways, each feeling the other's damned soul. At the gates of the passageway, Victor stops and turns to watch Carlo disappear into the darkness. Victor, a creature of darkness, is not fooled by Carlo's overnight success or his wicked air.

Soon after this chance meeting, both men again find themselves at the same public square where they were enchanted by Julieta. Both men have come in the hopes that their tormented souls will be serenaded by the blessed Julieta. This time, they do not remove their hats and instead greet each other with cold eyes.

Julieta walks next to the fountain in the humble square and removes her cloak. She then raises her head; with her eyes above the heads of those coming to a halt, she begins to sing. Carlo's adoring smile confirms to Victor that Carlo is infatuated with Julieta. Victor feels his blood boil, and he becomes struck with the realization that he too is enamored with Julieta. The sudden confirmation of feeling love for Julieta invigorates his soul. After escaping from Satan's claws in New Orleans, his dark heart has found light in a humble square filled with an angelic voice. Victor realizes that his damned heart is not completely dead. Falling in love with Julieta gives Victor hope for his damned soul. Victor waits for Julieta to take a bow, and then he exits the square. He does not want his competing presence to encourage Carlo to pursue Julieta. Victor needs to work with a cool head, not a boiling heart. The only man who can pose a challenge in his town is Carlo Fini. Victor refuses to allow Carlo's music to seduce the songstress. Victor can feel that Carlo is beaming with the confidence that he has the power to elevate Julieta's career and conquer her heart.

The next morning, Victor sends out his officials to locate Julieta and bring her to his mansion. Victor receives the apprehensive Julieta with a warm kiss on her trembling hand.

"Señor Montenegro, if I or my family caused a disturbance, I beg your pardon," Julieta says, feeling overwhelmed by the grand mansion and her private audience with the legendary illusionist.

"Disturbance?" Montenegro asks as he gallantly ushers her into the parlor.

"Yes, my singing in the plazas and squares."

Victor warmly motions her to sit down on an elegant couch. He sits down on the couch across from her.

"Your singing is not a disturbance. Your beautiful voice is a gift to our community."

"I hardly make enough to pay taxes," Julieta says regrettably.

Victor's gray eyes warmly look into her caramel eyes, and he assures her, "I do not want to tax you. I want to give you the stage you deserve."

Julieta's shoulders relax, and she smiles timidly at Victor.

"Stage?" Julieta whispers.

"Please join me for tea. I wish to know about you, about your family, and about your dreams."

Julieta looks at Victor's encouraging gray eyes, and she proclaims, "You were the kind and mysterious man with gray eyes who gave my brother three gold coins."

"Yes," Victor confirms.

Victor pours tea into the teacups and hands her one.

"Thank you, Señor Montenegro," Julieta says.

"You have a beautiful name. Would you mind terribly if…"

"I pray, please call me Julieta."

Victor warmly smiles at her and says, "Please tell me about yourself, Julieta."

"My mother was a rising star with a beautiful voice that touched many. We lost her, the world lost her, to consumption. My mother's parents sacrificed to be able to hire singing teachers, and just when she was making a name for herself, consumption silenced her forever."

"Your mother lives on in the beauty of your voice," Victor says.

"Thank you kindly."

"Consumption is a horrendous disease. I lost my beloved grandmother to consumption," Victor shares.

"Yes, I know. Her legacy lives on in the hospital that helps others," Julieta says.

"Yes, it does. Thank you," Victor says warmly.

Julieta reflects as their conversation continues. She strives to know her community intimately, and she feels that with her music, she has managed to connect with many in Montenegro as she ventures out after dusk to live her passion for singing and collect donations to help her family make ends meet. In her public performances, there are often familiar faces in the crowd. On occasion, she sees the silhouettes of prominent members of society who promenade through town secretly keeping to themselves in the audience, wishing to hear her songs but not be recognized. And she realizes that she occasionally has seen the silhouette of Victor where she is known to sing. Carlo Fini introducing himself to her was a highlight for her as an artist. Sitting in the Montenegro mansion—which is considered the heart of Montenegro itself—in private with the charismatic Victor Montenegro is an overwhelming honor.

Julieta is struck by the depths of his eyes that adore her. She can feel the energy of his soul. She shares the perception of many in her community who view Victor Montenegro as a mythical creature who resides in the grand mansion, developing his next mind-defying illusion. Outside of his mansion's gates, sightings of Victor are mainly consigned to city hall, a pew at the back of a church, and on a stage. Julieta feels timid and humble to have captured the attention of Victor Montenegro.

Victor can hear Julieta's heartbeat and the rhythmic ticking of the clock in the quietness of the parlor. He refills her tea and encourages her to select from the dessert cart.

"Forgive me, but why did you send for me?"

Victor looks down at the desserts and takes a moment to still his heart and fight his soul that begs him to declare his love for her. Victor clears his voice and asks, "Do you enjoy singing in the squares?"

"Do you enjoy performing in the plazas?" Julieta asks with a timid smile.

Victor looks into her eyes, and he smiles.

"Yes, but I also enjoy performing on a stage, where the audience is not rushed; they are in a comfortable setting where I can capture their complete attention."

"Yes," Julieta says with a yearning soul.

"I have stages throughout California at my disposal. And I am looking for an opening act. While I could feature fellow illusionists, I feel that opening up with your enchanting voice would be a gift to the audience. You are free to continue to sing in any plaza or public square. However, the stages across California will give you the recognition you dearly deserve. Recognition will afford you to take better care of your family. Your brother will be able to focus on school and discovering his own calling."

Victor studies the contemplating Julieta, and then he asks, "What does your father do?"

"He is an accountant, but he lost his business. I was away taking singing lessons. My father had to stop working to nurse my dying mother and look after my brother," Julieta says as tears escape her eyes.

Victor pulls his handkerchief from his breast pocket and hands it to Julieta.

Julieta, ignoring the napkin draped over her lap, takes his warm handkerchief and wipes her tears. "I beg your pardon," she whispers.

Victor is moved by the purity of her tears, and he says, "It is I who begs your pardon. I did not mean to upset you. Montenegro can use another accountant. Your father will work for the city. I will make sure that your brother attends school and has a nanny."

Victor looks at her lovingly as he encourages, "You can pursue your career as a singer."

Julieta clutches his handkerchief against her heart, and she says, "How can I repay you?"

"By singing for me. I mean, by being my opening act. You will be compensated and treated as a professional," Victor says.

Julieta's caramel eyes widen with anticipation, and she takes a cleansing breath and then promises, "With my compensation and my father working, my father and I will be able to pay for my brother's school and nanny."

"No. I do not want you and your father to worry. I will take care of your brother's education and nanny, as you will need to travel," Victor declares.

"This is awfully generous of you. I need to think of the best interest of my brother, and therefore I accept. In the future, I will find a way to compensate you."

"I do not want you to worry, Julieta. I want you to realize your dreams," Victor says.

There are no words to explain the joyousness Victor feels. He left New Orleans feeling like a walking corpse, with the only purpose in his life being to rescue his soul from the clutches of the devil. Darkness was his daily bread to keep him alive and out of hell. Outside of the warmth of his family and his ancestral home, he thought there would be no other joy. He had resigned himself to accepting that his life had ended on that forsaken hunt in the devil's seabed. Mourning for his mother was the only emotion his anguished soul could feel. Then, after one wrong turn, he walked into Julieta's world, and his heart was resurrected from darkness. Julieta is the light of his life. Like a rose needs the sun to bloom, Victor needs Julieta for his damned soul to flourish as it fights darkness. Julieta's agreeing to be his opening act revives his passion for large audiences, and Victor immediately hires a small group of handlers to book him and Julieta at the grand stages of California for prosperity and in small quaint venues to honor Julieta's love for intimate audiences.

Ernesto is relieved that Victor has awoken his passion for performing. Victor's self-imposed confinement to the mansion has cultivated much gossip. Ernesto has warned Victor that gossip can easily turn into fear and that fear can become active and destroy all that the Montenegro family has built and achieved. Sofia thanks God for giving Victor the courage to live and not just exist as she continues to attend daily mass to pray for the salvation of his soul.

Their First Show

The grand Montenegro Opera is a full house; all the seats and standing spots are taken. In attendance are the lucky audience members who were able to attain tickets for the first night of their week-long engagement and who will hear Montenegro's own songstress and watch Montenegro's own illusionist perform under the same roof. Also in attendance is Montenegro's celebrated violinist, Carlo, who sits in a balcony, compliments of Victor.

Julieta walks to the center of the stage. Carlo is mesmerized by her. In her elegant nightgown stands the humble beauty he has fallen in love with. Silence fills the opera house as the audience's eyes consume Julieta. As the orchestra begins to play, Julieta glances at Victor, who stands to off to the side, stage right. From behind a lush curtain, Victor encourages her with a warm smile and a nod. Julieta closes her eyes and begins to sing; the sound of her gifted voice filling up the opera house stuns her, and she looks over to Victor to ground her. Victor's enchanting eyes admiring her give her the confidence to continue her performance. Blinded by the spotlight, Julieta cannot clearly see the audience, but she can feel their presence, encompassing her with adoration. On the balcony, Carlo struggles with his desire for her. Her beautiful singing and the adoration of the audience endear her to him even more. As a performer himself, he is not a stranger to the stage his love is now singing from, and he is very aware of the spot where Victor is standing. And thus he knows that when Julieta looks in that direction, she is doing so to make eye contact with Victor. It burns Carlo to see Julieta seek out Victor for encouragement and strength to live out her passion. Carlo's only true desire is to be the one to care for her, to be there to encourage her and give her strength.

At the end of her performance, Victor does not move from his spot. He forbids the curtains to be lowered. Victor wants Julieta to benefit as much as she can from the adoring audience, who are on their feet, joyously clapping. Julieta takes in a gasp and steps back as she again looks toward Victor. Victor is smiling at her proudly and clapping. Julieta, visibly shaking with joy, focuses on the sound of Victor's clapping to steady herself in the exuberant wave of adoration from the audience. Her step back makes Victor fear that the overwhelming love of her public will make her swoon, so Victor joins her on the stage, his hands still clapping. He then grasps her hand to steady her as she takes a shaky but grateful bow. Carlo's hands are burning from his clapping.

It is tormenting Carlo's soul to watch Julieta rise from her last bow and see her eyes meet Victor's loving eyes as he kisses her hand. The gentle gesture causes the audience to erupt into another joyous round of applause that makes Carlo feel ill. The audience's encouragement of the warmth between Victor and Julieta fills Carlo with fear. Victor then steps away from Julieta, and as he stands far to her right, he opens his arms, and that gets the audience's attention. He then turns to face Julieta, and as he bows down to her, deep-red rose petals begin to rain down on her from directly above. The audience gasps with awe. Julieta, her eyes wide open, stands still as petals settle into the curls of her hair and gently cascade down her gown. Moved, she turns to face Victor, who smiles at her with admiration. At a loss for words, all she can do is smile. Victor lifts his arms, and the curtains fall when his arms do.

"Your performance was unmatched!" Victor congratulates her.

"Yes?" Julieta responds as she wonders if it is all a dream.

"It is not a dream. You were divine," Victor beams.

Victor's following performance captivates the audience, and Julieta is thrilled and mystified as she watches him perform from the side of the stage. She feels blessed to have shared the stage with the enchanting and mysterious Victor Montenegro. To close the show, Victor elevates a string quartet, and once in midair, the instruments play themselves, serenading the audience with a haunting melody. Carlo Fini feels that Victor's choice of the violins in his haunting melody is an acknowledgment that Victor knows about Carlo's dark contract.

Buried Gold

For years, Victor, along with every other citizen of Montenegro, had heard the persistent rumor that a Wells Fargo box with gold coins worth $80,000 is buried among the dead. It is believed that the buried loot belonged to the poetic robber nicknamed the Gentleman Bandit. The Gentleman Bandit was born Charles E. Boles in 1829 in England. With dreams of golden wealth, Boles rushed to California to mine. One day, two men pressured Boles to sell his mine to them. Boles strongly declined the offer, as he was confident the mine had gold. The men who wanted his mine were connected to Wells Fargo. Wells Fargo was establishing its lines in mining towns, and there was talk that Wells Fargo was going into the mining business, and this made Boles suspicious. Wells Fargo diverted the water of the stream running through Boles's claim, water that he needed to mine for gold. Without any water, Boles had no other choice but to abandon his mine. Boles was furious with Wells Fargo, and he promised, "I am going to take steps."

Boles concocted a genius plan. Rifle in hand, he stood in the middle of a road along a Wells Fargo route. The road had trees and bushes on each side. Within the trees and bushes, he strategically situated sticks to look like they were rifles. As a Wells Fargo coach came to a halt at the end of Boles's rifle, Boles quickly glanced toward the sticks and instructed, "Hold your fire." Wearing a flour sack with eye holes over his head, Boles instructed the coachman, "Please drop down the Wells Fargo box." A woman in the stagecoach, frightened, threw her purse out the window onto the ground. Boles picked up the purse, respectfully bowed to her, handed the purse back to her, and said, "Madam, I do not wish your money. In that respect, I honor only the good office of Wells Fargo." Boles was legendary for being very courteous to the passengers of Wells Fargo. Boles was especially courteous to female travelers, always refusing to take their money and jewels. Boles, the Gentleman Bandit, avoided gunfights, and instead of leaving bloodshed, he would leave poems, which made an impression among the stagecoach drivers.

On November 3, 1883, Sheriff Tom Cunningham examined the area where the Sonora stagecoach was held up by Boles. On the ground, he found a handkerchief with the laundry mark *FX07*. Harry Morse, of the Morse Patrol Detective Agency of San Francisco, found the same marks on other linens in a San Francisco laundry. When Morse visited the laundry to inquire about the marks, the proprietor was in the midst of telling him that the marked linens belonged to a valued customer when Boles walked in to collect his laundry.

Boles pleaded guilty to the charge of stagecoach robbery, and he was sentenced to a term at San Quentin prison on November 21, 1833. Before his sentencing, Boles handed over some of his loot to another infamous stagecoach robber for safekeeping. The stagecoach robber hid Boles's loot alongside some of his loot in a San Francisco cemetery, banking on religion and respect for the dead to guard the loot.

The only souls who dare to disturb cemetery dirt are grave robbers whose mission is to steal the corpses from fresh graves to sell to doctors, who pay handsomely for the recently departed. The fear of cemetery dirt, fertilized with the pain of suffering and cursed by the dark work of witches, being tracked into a home is terrifying enough. However, it is the fear that a demon from a wicked departed looking for a living host that prevents people from seeking the cemetery treasure of the never-dying legend of Black Bart's buried loot.

No one can say with certainty what became of Boles after he was released from prison. The robber who buried the loot in the San Francisco cemetery met his demise when the law caught up with him in another town. The sheriff's faster draw caught the robber between the eyes, and he dropped dead on top of the grave of his late mother. The fact that the robber was killed in a cemetery increased the fear of the cemetery loot being cursed, and thus it remained undisturbed in 1905.

Victor Montenegro, whose interest in treasure hunting had been piqued by Ivan's lifelong passion, found himself considering the tale anew. Out of respect for the sanctity of hollow ground and not having any desire to gamble with evil, he previously would not have sought out the legendary cemetery loot. But things changed when he returned from New Orleans. A demon cannot claim what the devil himself has already marked. Victor's run-in with the devil has replaced his guarded respect for evil with unbridled rivalry, which now inspires in him the desire to claim the cemetery loot.

San Francisco, 1905

On a warm fall morning, Victor Montenegro and Julieta Maria Avila arrive in San Francisco to perform for a year-long engagement. Victor Montenegro has reserved two suites in the St. Francis Hotel, which opened its doors on March 21, 1904. Julieta is awed by the grand hotel and appreciative of her personal suite, but she feels that Victor is being too extravagant. Victor celebrates the golden accommodations and world-renowned service of the St. Francis, but more important to him is that the hotel was named after a saint.

After a scrumptious dinner, Victor escorts Julieta to her suite so she can rest her voice in preparation for the following night's performance.

Victor strolls from the St. Francis Hotel to Union Square, and under the shadow of the Victory Monument, which was dedicated by Theodore Roosevelt in 1903, he transforms into a bat and takes flight, soaring into the San Francisco fog. He flies over a cemetery's locked gates and lands on the mound of a fresh grave. He walks off the mound and then transforms into his human form. He begs the recently departed a pardon, and he strolls between the tombstones, his senses amplified. He tours most of the cemetery, and his senses do not locate the loot. Disappointed, he sits down on the steps of a mausoleum. As he thinks about which other cemetery he should visit next, his eyes fall on a headstone bearing the name of a late female, under which *My treasure* is written in Spanish. Victor walks over to the grave, and he is struck by the smell of gold. He removes his hat and bows. As Victor straightens up, he catches the moon shining off a shovel resting next to a grave that was robbed of its body. Victor raises his hand in the direction of the shovel, and the shovel glides above the hallowed ground and into Victor's commanding open hand.

It does not take long for the shovel to hit a wooden trunk. Victor lifts the trunk out of hiding and places it on the ground. With his hand, he channels the heat from his body to explode the lock open. Inside the trunk, there are three unmarked sacks filled with gold, and perched in the middle of two sacks is a piece of paper. He unfolds the paper and reads, *In Heaven souls walk on gold. From Hell souls are bought with gold. On Earth gold could pave your way to walk on gold, or boil in a cauldron made out of gold.*

Victor walks to the cemetery's locked gates. He then deploys his bat wings. Carrying the wooden trunk, he flies over the gates. On the street, he spots a coach. Approaching the coach, he asks the driver if he is available for hire. The coachman responds that he is available, puts down his sketchbook and pencils, and jumps down to assist Victor. The coachman, recognizing the famous illusionist, asks, "A lovely evening, isn't it, my good sir?"

"Indeed, I found Black Bart's treasure," Victor proudly proclaims.

"Not only are you the spitting image of your late father, may he rest in peace, but you also inherited his luck for finding elusive treasures and his power to perform illusions," says the awestruck coachman.

"What is your name, my good man?"

"Stewart Van Green."

"Are you a family man, Mr. Van Green?"

"No, sir."

"I am in need of a private coachman. I will compensate you very well on and off the clock for your devoted service and discretion."

"Yes! At your service, Mr. Montenegro."

※

Victor will heed the poem he found in the treasure box. Victor, whose own fortune far outweighs the loot in the trunk, is not interested in making a profit; rather, he aims to perpetuate his family's history of generous philanthropists.

The first thing the following morning, he invites the *San Francisco Chronicle* and the *San Francisco Examiner* to St. Francis. In a meeting with the journalists, he declares, "In keeping with the spirit of St. Francis of Assisi, whom this great city was named after, I will evenly divide the cemetery loot among the poor citizens of San Francisco."

Victor receives countless words of praise and is celebrated by all in San Francisco for his generosity. Victor banks on the support of the San Francisco citizens and the national coverage to prevent legal action regarding the treasure. The trunk is unmarked, the sacks are unmarked, and although there was a poem in the treasure, the poem was not signed by Black Bart. Because the treasure is not clearly marked, no agencies have legal right to claim the loot. And if they were to try to claim the treasure, this could easily ruin them in the eyes of the public because it would seem as though they want to take from the poor.

Victor assigns the post of distributing the money to the poor to Julieta's accountant father. Julieta is moved and thrilled that Victor has special consideration and trust for her father. Donating the treasure to the poor greatly enhances Victor's public image. People pour into San Francisco to see Victor and Julieta perform. Victor's national press gets the attention of Carlo Fini.

"Why isn't Julieta Maria Avila enthralled by me? Why isn't Julieta Maria Avila at my command?" Carlo demands.

"Julieta Maria Avila's name is not on the contract. You have an ocean of women who worship you as a legendary musician, and they all would love to be your muse, your lover. I said women. I did not promise you Julieta Maria Avila," the dark one replies as he slithers away, his guttural laughter thundering through Carlo's elegant mansion.

Carlo soon arrives in San Francisco and buys a ticket to every one of Victor and Julieta's shows. Carlo rages with jealousy that Julieta shares the spotlight with Victor. Carlo is angry that Julieta is not performing with him.

One evening, after another sublime performance, Carlo Fini rises to his feet to accompany the standing ovation. Carlo's clapping echoes from the balcony. Carlo's adoration is not lost on the audience members, who slightly turn to face Carlo and greet him with applause. Julieta looks in the direction of the audience, acknowledges Carlo with a smile, and then casts her eyes toward Victor, who materializes a rose from the air and hands it to her. Carlo smiles to hide his jealousy from the adoring audience.

Not a stranger to the theater, Carlo walks unannounced to the back of the stage to personally congratulate Victor and Julieta on their performance. As he approaches them, he witnesses the enchantment in Julieta's eyes as Victor enthralls her by producing, out of thin air, two diamond hair combs for her chocolate locks and hands them to her as a token of appreciation for their continued highly sought-out San Francisco performances. Carlo announces himself by applauding Victor's magical gesture.

"Good evening, Mr. Fini. Did you enjoy our show?" Victor asks Carlo as Carlo's eyes feast on Julieta as she delicately places the combs in her hair.

Without removing his eyes from Julieta, he answers, "I did indeed—magnificent."

Carlo takes Julieta's free hand into his and bows to kiss her hand, then he says, "You were sublime. There never was nor will there ever be a singer like you."

"You are very kind, Mr. Fini. Thank you," Julieta responds.

"I would like to invite you two out for breakfast," Carlo Fini says.

"Our performing engagements, the late dinners, and the parties that follow keep us up until dawn. We slumber through breakfast," Victor explains.

"What a dreadful schedule," Carlo says to Julieta.

"Not at all. As a performer, I have always been accustomed to living at night and sleeping during the day," Julieta responds.

"Of course. As a performer, I understand," Carlo says.

"You are more than welcome to join us on one of these evenings, but tonight Julieta and I will be at a private cocktail at the senator's home," Victor says as he extends his arm out to Julieta. Julieta settles her hand into the bend of Victor's arm.

"Tell me, has the San Francisco fog eased your migraine suffering?" Carlo asks.

Victor's eyes impale Carlo's eyes with suspicion, and then he answers, "Yes, indeed. The fog blocks the bright sun, which helps immensely. But I hope that I will find a cure for my sensitivity to light and not always be a creature of the dark. We are all creatures of the light, and we should not live in darkness."

"Good night, Mr. Fini. Thank you for gracing our performance with your presence," Julieta says.

Carlo removes his top hat and bows to her. Julieta turns to face the exit, Victor turns to look at Carlo, and the two men exchange glances of contempt as Victor leads Julieta away.

Carlo watches as the diamonds in the combs that Victor gave her twinkle as Julieta follows Victor through the lit area of the backstage toward the exit. Carlo shakes with envy toward Victor and anger at himself. His lack of control allowed for his feelings of contempt toward Victor to saturate his body language and tone. Now, he fears that he has awakened the demon in Victor by alluding that he is aware of his nature by asking Victor about his migraines. The evil that dwells in Carlo gives him the privy to know that Victor is a vampire and that he uses the excuse of suffering from migraines to explain his lack of sunny outings.

Christmas, 1905

Victor's family joins Victor in San Francisco to spend Christmas season with him and watch his performance, which has captured the attention of all San Franciscans. Victor's early Christmas present to Julieta is to pay for her father and brother to travel to San Francisco and stay at the St. Francis Hotel. Carlo Fini decides to spend the holidays in San Francisco to perform and stay close to the love of his life, Julieta.

The adoration and warmth in Victor's eyes for Julieta warms Sofia's heart. One night after a scrumptious dinner, Sofia pulls Victor aside and says to him, "Dear brother, it is undeniable that you have fallen in love with Julieta. The greatest gift that God gave us..."

"Free will," Victor says.

"No. Love. Love is what connects us to God. Love is a great gift, and so is romantic love. The fact that you can fall in love says that you are not completely separated from God. Do not give up on love. Embrace that love you have for her. Honor love. Live with love in your heart, mind, and soul, and by doing so, you will honor God."

Victor bows his head with respect to his younger sister; her devotion to praying for the salvation of his soul is beyond measure. Victor then looks into his sister's eyes as he takes her hands and places them against his chest. As his sister feels his heart thumping against his chest, Victor says to her with regret, "My heart is not whole."

Sofia looks up at her brother, and confusion fills her eyes. The joy she expects to see in his eyes is not present. The pain in his eyes overwhelms her. She presses her hands against his chest as she hides her worry and studies him.

"My heart is not whole. The human side of me is blessed with the ability to fall in love. The monster side of me curses me to never have the blessings of true mutual love."

"But, I see how Julieta..."

"Julieta has affection, respect, and, above all, immense gratitude for me. But not love—it will never be the love I desire."

Sofia fights her tears as she argues, "Nonsense. You are a handsome man of substance, powerful, caring, and enchanting."

Victor smiles, "Why, thank you, sister."

"I am deadly serious. There is no reason a woman like her cannot fall in love with you. She has become quite your shadow, always happy to be anchored on your arm. As a woman, I can read the attraction she has for you."

"Attraction is not love, dear sister. Each sweet smile she gifts me feeds my soul, but my heart hungers for more. I have to accept my dark fate. I pray that from her attraction and her immense gratitude, affection will grow."

"While attraction and gratitude still dwell in her heart for you, propose to her! She will accept. Only a madwoman would say no to Victor Montenegro, the grand illusionist and diplomat with a heart of gold."

Victor pulls away from his sister and says, "No. I will not deny her love. Love is the greatest gift. She deserves mutual love, and by marrying me, it will cheat her out of the greatest gift."

"Perhaps she is the type of woman who prefers security over love."

"Perhaps," Victor agrees for the sake of his sister.

"Pay close attention to Julieta. When a woman is set on marrying someone, she will clue in the gentleman."

"Perhaps," Victor repeats again.

Christmas Mass Celebration

The holiday and the Christmas festivities do not deter Sofia from her devotion in praying for the salvation of Victor's soul. Every day, Sofia attends Mass at Saint Francis of Assisi, which was established in 1849 for Catholics who came to California to seek their golden fortune and was dedicated in 1860. On days when her brothers do not protest, Sofia attends the English, Spanish, and Italian masses. Victor is filled with guilt that she prays every day for him instead of living the life God has given her. Ernesto, time and time again, for the sake of her well-being pleads with her that she should only attend Mass once a day.

"Praying for his salvation daily is taxing, but to plead thrice a day must be taxing to God, as if you do not trust that he heard you the first time," Ernesto advises Sofia.

"I know he hears me, and I ask God that for each hour of Mass I pray, Victor will be spared a month in hell," Sofia says.

"He is a vampire. He has no risk of dying and plunging into hell. He will survive us. When your time comes, you can take your petition directly to God in his heavenly home."

Victor's whole family celebrates midnight Christmas mass. Victor takes his usual place in the last row of the church, as far away as possible from the brilliance of the crucifix, which causes Victor's unholy body burning pain. In the back pew, elegantly dressed in a black suit with a red tie, he kneels, and as the reflections of the flickering candles hanging above him waltz on his dark glasses, he prays for peace and strength for his sister Sofia, who has been carrying his cross.

After midnight mass, the family exchanges gifts. Victor presents Sofia with a picture of a new birdhouse, with room for many nests that he commissioned and had installed in the garden of her home. "This is such a beautiful dovecot! I absolutely love it! Thank you for your very thoughtful gift!" Sofia says as she embraces her brother.

"You love it when the turtledoves visit your garden, and now they can move in. I never understood your passion for turtledoves," Victor says.

"Turtledoves are a symbol of love. Turtledoves mate for life, and they are known to mourn their mates," Sofia says.

"Beautiful," is all that Victor can say.

"I believe you found your turtledove—Julieta."

"May God hear you, sister," Victor whispers.

"It was very thoughtful of you to send for her family to spend Christmas with her. I am sure she thinks about you with every grateful word from her father and every hug from her little brother," Sofia says.

At three in the afternoon on Christmas Day, Victor jolts awake. With a heavy and racing heart, Victor quickly dresses as he tries to shake the uneasy feeling of death. Victor pounds on the door of the suite of his visiting family.

"You will wake up the dead with that pounding!" Ernesto protests.

Victor pushes past him into the suite.

"What in the devil is wrong?" Ernesto demands.
"Is everyone here?" Victor asks.
"The kids are taking a stroll in the Union Square."
"Where is Sofia?" Victor asks.
They rush to Sofia's closed bedroom door, and Ernesto knocks. No answer.
"Quickly, brother," Victor begs.

As they rush into the church of Saint Francis of Assisi, they are struck by the gentle scent of roses perfumed with melting candle wax. The flickering candle flames glow in the dimmed church. In the middle of the aisle, they freeze. They see the silhouette of their sister sitting in the front pew, bathed in a ray of sunlight tunneling down from a magnificent stained-glass window. Each can feel the other's soul shudder; each hears the pounding of his heart. The brilliance of the light prevents Victor from racing to her, as Ernesto does. Victor watches as Ernesto's hand loses the grip on his hat and it drops silently onto the floor. Ernesto contemplates his younger sister, bathed in the brilliant ray of sunlight. Her body's rigidity confirms her death, but her face is not the mask of death. A sweet smile is upon her face, as if she is enjoying a lovely dream. Ernesto picks his sister up into his arms, the sun ray disappears, and Victor drops to his knees.

"Why did you take the only light of my life!" Victor demands as he rips his dark glasses from his eyes.

Victor gets up and races to Ernesto. He takes Sofia from Ernesto's embrace and cradles her in his arms as blood tears rain down on her.

"She is in peace. She died with a sweet smile upon her lips, her face looking younger and very beautiful. There is no doubt in my mind that it was not the angel of death that came for her, but an archangel must have ascended for her," Ernesto comforts.

Victor, through his blood tears, contemplates his sister in his arms as Ernesto goes to order Stewart to pull up the coach to the entry of the church.

"Rest in peace, my beloved sister, while I pray that we shall meet again in the light," Victor cries.

Sofia's daughters have the task of changing their late mother's dress, which is stained by their uncle's blood tears. They console one another with the thought that their mother died in God's house and that now she is in heaven, reunited with their father, her late husband.

Doctors are at a loss to explain Sofia's death. She was last seen alive during midday mass, and as usual, she stayed in church after Mass had ended. A few parishioners who entered the church to pray saw her kneeling in prayer. At the end of the investigation, the coroner declares that she died from exhaustion.

Victor locks himself in his suite and allows himself to bleed his pain out in his tears. No one outside of the family can see him cry blood. Sofia's death is not a mystery to him.

"I prayed for your peace. And peace was given to you," Victor realizes out loud.

"I prayed for your peace, not your death. I am sure you are now in Heaven; you were a godly woman," Victor says.

Julieta accompanies Victor and his family back to Montenegro to lay Sofia to rest. Montenegro citizens mourn the passing of their beloved Sofia for three days.

Julieta is overwhelmed with compassion for Victor. The profound sadness in Victor is painful for Julieta. Julieta, wishing to comfort him and distract him from his loss, stays at his side on and off the stage.

After a few days of mourning, Victor and Julieta return to San Francisco to resume their performance engagements. Carlo Fini personally express his condolences to Victor. Carlo is disturbed and threatened by Julieta's warm and constant attention to Victor. Carlo fears that Julieta's compassion for Victor will grow into love. The grief in Victor's eyes dismisses Carlo's suspicion that Sofia was sacrificed by Victor in order to garner Julieta's devotion and affection.

Carlo is invited to attend a gala dinner hosted by the governor of California. Among the dinner party of fifty guests are Victor and Julieta. As the dinner guests enjoy the governor's favorite meal of deviled oysters, roasted turkey, caviar sandwiches, potatoes, and green peas, Carlo and Victor barely touch their respective meals; instead, their eyes feast on Julieta as she enjoys her dinner. Love sickness for Julieta robs Carlo of his appetite. Carlo's presence at the dinner and his distaste for fowl rob Victor of his appetite.

Victor is glad that he drank fresh animal blood at the slaughterhouse earlier that day. Bloodletting is no longer in practice, and Victor tires of hunting for rodents in undesirable neighborhoods, which has resulted in Victor frequenting slaughterhouses for his nutritional needs. Incognito, Victor shows up at a slaughterhouse and stands in line with consumption sufferers who are seeking a cure and those without consumption who are hoping to stave off the dreaded sickness. It is believed that drinking the warm blood of slaughtered animals will cure those who suffer from the bloody disease. The suffering and fear of the people in the queue for fresh blood pains

Victor. He, however, is not suffering from the horrible disease that is consuming hundreds of people; he must drink blood to give him the strength and vitality to perform.

As Julieta sips her red wine, Carlo raises his wine and wonders if Julieta is in love with Victor. Victor washes down the contempt he feels for Carlo with his wine. The only worthy competitor for Victor's heart's desire is Carlo. Victor worries that Julieta's free heart will be wooed by Carlo's musical charms.

After dinner, as the guests enjoy one another's company, the governor sequesters Victor in his private office to talk about diplomatic matters. Carlo graciously declines the orchestra's invitation to play with them. Holding his violin, he follows Julieta out to the mansion's grand balcony. She turns to the sound of the balcony doors closing.

"Forgive me. I wrongly assumed no one else is out here. I closed the doors to silence the chatter so I can take a moment to contemplate the stars in silence," Carlo says.

"It is a beautiful evening," Julieta says as she extends her hand to him.

Carlo gratefully takes her hand and presses the back of it against his forehead, and then he kisses her hand and declares, "You look lovely tonight. I hope you are enjoying the evening."

"Yes, I am. A new world has opened up to me, and I am very grateful. I see you have your violin," Julieta says, smiling.

"I pray, let me play something for you, my lady."

Carlo begins to play, and his violin rings out a melody that no one else's ears have ever heard, not even his. Carlo's own amazement for the new melody is dwarfed by the enchantment on Julieta's face as each cell in her being takes in the notes that pour from maestro Carlo Fini's violin.

The melody takes flight and streams into the open balcony of the governor's office, burning into Victor's ears.

"A beautiful melody. Maestro Fini is the greatest musician alive," the governor says.

A dark chill plunges through Victor's heart. Carlo's violin possesses the ability to enchant all mortals.

The governor, holding on to his brandy, walks closer to the open balcony doors and listens to the melody. Victor glares into the governor's eyes.

"Forgive me. You know, politicians have the power. We are revered out of fear. Women only seek our affection for the protection. Being a politician is a lonely station. Adoration, respect, and love are reserved for those who can enchant souls. Carlo Fini and you, Don Victor Montenegro, are gifted with the ability to enchant souls," the governor laments as he walks out to the balcony and looks down. On the grand balcony below, he sees Carlo serenading Julieta.

"Maestro Carlo is serenading Lady Julieta. I would love to hear her sing along to his divine melody," the governor says.

Victor, fighting to contain himself, walks to stand next to the governor and looks down at the scene. The enchantment in Julieta's eyes sears his heart with pain.

Unbeknownst to the governor, Victor commands the doors on their balcony to lock. Then Victor commands the strings of Carlo's violin to pop out of place, ending his melody. Juliet, in disbelief, looks at the mangled violin strings.

"It seems my song was too emotional for my violin," Carlo says with a smile.

"It is the most moving melody I've ever heard," Julieta professes.

"Having your audience is a great honor. I pray, accept my invitation to dinner, and I will play for you again."

Julieta silently contemplates his pleading eyes, then she says with regret, "My schedule will not permit me to accept your invitation. I am committed to my performances with Señor Montenegro; without him, I would still be performing in public squares."

"Yes, Montenegro has done you a great service. A service that

I too can offer you. I would be the most grateful man if you would grace my stage with your gifted voice."

"It would be an honor, but I do not know where the future will take me. Thank you kindly for the offer," Julieta says as she walks toward the balcony doors.

Carlo rushes to the doors to open them for her. The doors do not open.

"I fear that someone has locked the doors without realizing we are out here," Carlo says with a comforting smile.

Julieta's knocks against the doors are drowned out by the orchestra inside. Julieta turns to Carlo and looks at him with panicked eyes.

"We will wait for the orchestra to end their song, and we will knock again. Do not worry, my lady," Carlo assures her as he wraps his jacket around her shoulders.

Julieta holds the lapels of his coat as she walks to the balcony railing. She hears the governor conversing on the balcony above theirs.

"Governor, we are locked out," she calls out to him.

Victor climbs over the railing and drops to the balcony below. Julieta jumps, startled, and then she smiles.

"Forgive me. I did not mean to startle you. The doors are locked?" Victor says as he looks at Carlo's jacket on her shoulders with disdain.

"Yes, Mr. Fini…"

"Carlo," Carlo insists.

"Carlo tried to open the doors, to no avail," Julieta says.

Victor snaps his fingers once, the balcony doors open, and the orchestra's music floods out.

Julieta's shoulders relax, and she beams a smile.

"Thank you!" Julieta says as she passes Victor, moving toward the open doors.

"Permit me," Victor pleads, and with his hand, he commands Carlo's jacket to lift off her shoulders. Julieta looks over her shoulder at Carlo's jacket suspended in the air, and she giggles into the palm of her hand. Victor's hand commands the jacket to fly to Carlo, and the jacket crashes against Carlo's face.

"Pardon me. It is a trick I am still perfecting," Victor says to Carlo with a tight jaw.

Carlo grabs his coat, and as he puts it over his arm, he says, "An illusionist with a sense of humor."

"I am glad I amuse you. Good night, Fini," Victor responds as he extends his bent arm to Julieta and escorts her back inside.

Capturing a Song

"Julieta will be mine," Carlo declares. The flame of the candle in front of him snaps and hisses. Carlo, feeling cold, pours himself a snifter of brandy.

As he sips his drink, his chest tightens. The flame of the candle sways and dances in the cold darkness. "I must woo her before she falls in love with that damned Montenegro," Carlo muses.

"Two damned souls battling for the love of a songstress with an angelic voice," a voice in the darkness says with a growling laugh.

"One way or another, she will be mine," Carlo yells into the darkness.

"Tall order," the voice says.

"I must find a way to capture her heart before she falls in love with the insufferable Montenegro!"

"She will never fall in love with Montenegro."

"What?" Carlo eagerly questions.

"Montenegro is in love with your beloved. Montenegro is damned; mutual love is forbidden."

Carlo laughs hysterically, and then he angrily says, "I put no weight on your words. You are ruled by the father of lies. Do not torture me with false hope."

The dark mass takes the shape of a dapperly dressed man with the head of a goat sitting across the table from Carlo. Carlo keeps his eyes on his brandy.

"Julieta is the most beautiful creature I have ever seen. She has a heart of gold and a voice of an angel. Julieta's light feeds my soul."

Carlo ignores the evil stare of the goat's black eyes.

"Julieta inspires my heart. The song I serenaded her with was born on that balcony. My love for her created a melody for her. I felt her soul that night through my melody."

"Yes, you are gifted," the black-eyed goat mocks.

"No! My love for her is pure, and so is the melody I composed on the balcony for her. Montenegro's astute plan to have her tour with him is a ruse to keep her at his side. Julieta is comfortable around him, and she is spellbound by him."

"Yes, she is blind to his darkness. It is an illusion," the goat says, laughing.

"Why are you here?" Carlo demands.

"She will never fall in love with you, Carlo. While alive, Julieta will be bound to Montenegro by her gratitude for his support, her admiration for his standing on the international stage, and his captivating illusions."

"While alive?" Carlo questions.

"Certainly, a soul as pure as hers will never feel the fires of hell," the monster digresses.

"She inspired me to create a melody beyond my inspiration. I desperately need her by my side. My heart demands it. My soul has no comfort without her. She is my violin."

"You will never be the owner of her heart."

"What do you know about love?" Carlo retorts.

The room gets ice cold, and Carlo shivers as he says, "I want her light to inspire me. I need her by my side as my muse."

"Is that a wish?" the goat asks, and then it materializes a snifter of fire and clinks it against Carlo's snifter.

Suzette fears that the sound of the pounding of her heart will break through the silence of Victor's captivated audience. Victor puts Julieta to sleep and then rests her on air. As Victor holds a large ring steady, the sleeping Julieta passes through the ring, her flowing hair and dress gently caressing the bottom of the ring. As her body remains suspended, Victor tosses up the ring, and it disappears. Standing in front of the sleeping Julieta, he pauses to contemplate her peaceful face. As Victor raises his arms, Julieta's sleeping body slowly ascends above. He removes his black cloak and twirls it up to spread out a few inches under the suspended Julieta. From Julieta's cascading hair, roses rain down, spreading out like water onto his black cloak. The audience, mesmerized by the shower of roses, fails to notice that Julieta's body disappears from sight. The shower of roses stops. Victor raises his arms up, and a collective gasp fills the theater as the audience's eyes search the stage for the missing Julieta. The black cloak remains suspended in the air, sustaining a bed of roses two feet high. At the command of Victor's hand, the cloak folds to conceal the bed of roses. Victor stretches out his arms, and the folded cloak drops to his outstretched arms. Victor's arms curl the cloak with roses toward his chest, and then he quickly extends his arms to reveal that he is now holding the smiling Julieta, who is wearing his cloak.

All in the audience jump to their feet. The pounding sound of Suzette's heart breaking is drowned out by the uproarious adoration of the audience.

The knock on his door hits his heart, then he looks up to see Suzette standing between him and his locked door. Suzette raises her hand to him, and he graciously kisses her gloved hand.

"Pleasant surprise that you are in town," Victor says.

"News of your celebrated performances travels quickly. There are no words to describe your ability to enthrall audiences."

Victor gently hangs the cloak that materialized Julieta.

"It is nothing more than showmanship and dark control of the elements," Victor utters.

"Nonsense, my love. You are a great illusionist. Had I known you were in the market for an assistant, I would've moved land and earth to tour with you. The songstress's gift is to sing, not to enchant as only you and I can."

"You have your responsibilities in New Orleans, and I…"

"And you are in love with her," Suzette says, trembling.

"Please, do not make this difficult," Victor pleads.

"I have no rights over your heart," Suzette says. "She is very talented, and you two complement each other."

"It is lovely to see you. You look great," Victor says, giving her a warm hug.

"I will need a feeding in a couple of days. I am not familiar with the streets of San Francisco. Bloodletting therapy slowly died under the suspicion that it was bloodletting that killed George Washington."

Victor repeats George Washington's dying words: "Doctor, I die hard; but I am not afraid to go; I believed from my first attack that I should not survive it; my breath cannot last long."

Victor pauses and looks down. Suzette can feel his mind thinking about blood.

Victor looks up and studies Suzette, and then he asks, "If a vampire is drained of all its blood, will it kill it?"

"It?" Suzette questions.

"What would happen?"

"My love, we are still creatures of God."

"Please, tell me, what would happen?"

"It will not destroy the vampire, but the vampire will become a zombie vampire. A vampire needs iron to be able to function like a human; without iron, we are just living…"

"Things," Victor finishes.

"Living creatures without the ability to reason as we normally do," Suzette says.

Victor nods. He walks over to the bar and pours them both some brandy.

Graciously taking the brandy, Suzette then asks, "How do you feed?"

"It has been mainly rodents; lately, I have been visiting slaughterhouses for fresh, warm blood."

"That sounds delicious, but are you not afraid of being recognized?"

"The poor souls in line for blood are too weak or frightened of consumption to take note of who else is in line with them. However, I go in disguise so that the butchers will not recognize me."

"That sounds fun—incognito, we shall devour warm blood from a fresh kill!"

"We will go together to fetch blood. But now I need to excuse myself. Julieta and I are expected at a charity gala at the St. Francis," Victor says.

The gala is lively and grand. Victor and Julieta enter the main ballroom and are received with uproarious applause. Carlo looks at the celebrated couple, and he feels defrauded. The arrival of Victor dims his celebrity glow. The attentive manner in which Victor shares the limelight with Julieta wounds his ego. Julieta, her arm anchored on Victor's bent arm, is light on her feet. The guests gather around them. A timid Julieta looks at Victor and tenderly smiles at him. Carlo's heart breaks with envy. Victor and Julieta approach Carlo.

Victor extends his hand to Carlo, which Carlo firmly shakes.

"Mr. Fini, how do you do?" Victor asks.

"Splendid, Mr. Montenegro."

Carlo drops Victor's hand and extends his open palm to Julieta. Julieta places her hand in his palm. "Mr. Fini," she acknowledges.

Carlo bows and kisses her hand, and without releasing her hand, he pleads again, "Carlo."

Julieta smiles at him in agreement.

"You are ever so beautiful, my lady," Carlo says.

"Thank you, you are very kind. Are you enjoying your evening?"

"Indeed," Carlo says, smiling.

"Excuse us," Victor interrupts.

Victor gives an encouraging smile to Julieta and explains, "I wish to introduce you to Mayor Eugene E. Schimtz before he departs for the evening."

A lady approaches them, and as the lady engages Julieta, Carlo leans in toward Victor and argues, "Schimtz allegedly is corrupt! Julieta does not need to know the likes of him."

"Is Schimtz a corrupt musician?" Victor asks with contempt in his voice.

"Allegedly, a corrupt politician," Carlo fumes.

"An allegedly corrupt politician is easier to wrangle than a damned soul," Victor says.

The lady departs, and then Julieta studies the indifferent stance between Victor and Carlo.

"Out of concern for you, Mr. Fini objects that I introduce you to Mayor Schimtz, a fellow musician of his. But I assured Mr. Fini that no harm will come from meeting the mayor, or anyone else for that matter, as I will not permit it," Victor promises.

Victor takes a couple of tickets for their next performance out of his breast pocket and hands them to Carlo, "My compliments. Good night, Mr. Fini."

"It was delightful seeing you again," Julieta says to Carlo as she allows Victor to guide her away from him.

As much as it pains him not to be the one at Julieta's side, Carlo refuses to leave the gala. He wants Victor to feel him shadowing him. He mingles with the guests so Julieta can witness firsthand that, like Victor, he too garners the admiration and adoration of the distinguished guests.

Victor and Julieta stroll through two ornate rooms dressed with large windows that showcase the beautiful evening and opulent gardens. In the third room, where the orchestra is playing, Victor and Julieta are greeted by the mayor. Victor introduces Julieta to Mayor Schimtz, who is charmed by their presence.

"It is such a privilege for our community to be enchanted by the two of you," Schimtz says with open arms.

At the supplication of the orchestra's conductor and to the delight of the guest, the mayor and Carlo are persuaded to play with the orchestra. Mayor Schimtz, an accomplished violin player, looks at Carlo and hesitates; he does not relish having to share the stage with the legendary Carlo. Carlo bows and encourages the mayor to join him on the stage.

Silence falls over the ballroom as everyone in attendance locks their eyes on the orchestra and holds their breath with anticipation. The members of the orchestra nervously ready their respective instruments. Carlo holds his violin against his chest as he relishes the amusement in Julieta's eyes as she observes how the members of the orchestra, one by one, exhale to calm their excitement of sharing the stage with the living legend Carlo Fini.

The conductor consults with Carlo regarding which song he would like to be accompanied by, and Carlo answers for all to hear, "I shall lead you."

The fear of inability projected from the eyes of all the members of the orchestra, including the ever confident Mayor Schimtz, is observed by the guests.

Julieta covers her lips with her fan and discreetly giggles. She looks back up at the stage and meets Carlo's eyes, and he says, "In your honor, Madame Julieta."

Carlo places his violin under his chin, and the members of the orchestra hold their breath, anxious to interpret his first note. Carlo raises his bow, and the members nervously await the tune. Carlo begins to play, and the orchestra and the mayor begin to follow the melody. The guests look at one another with awe in their eyes that their ears are being treated to a new song. The attention of the guests is on the stage; the ballroom's marble floor is undisturbed by dancing feet.

Victor stands behind Julieta, and over her bare shoulder, he observes Carlo. Carlo continues to lead the orchestra and the mayor in his passionate melody—a melody new to Victor's ear, but not to his soul. Victor can feel the hand of the beast in every note and on every string, key, and horn. Victor lifts Julieta's hand and kisses it. She glances back at him with dreamy eyes, as if she is in a trance. He twirls her around to face him. He bows and then takes her into a dancer's embrace and begins to waltz with her. Their elegant waltz breaks the spell of the melody, and she says to Victor, "Dancing with you is like waltzing on air."

The guests circle around the waltzing couple. Victor bows his head, smiles, and then says, "We are waltzing on air."

Julieta sees the amazement in the eyes of the guests around them, and she slowly looks down to see that they are waltzing two feet above the floor. Julieta tightens her grip on Victor's hand and anchors her other hand tighter on his shoulder.

In a calm and confident tone, Victors instructs, "Julieta, look at me."

Julieta's frightened eyes lock on Victor's confident eyes.

With a gentle smile, he says, "I have you. Do not fear. I will never put you in harm's way."

Julieta lightens her grip on his hand, relaxes her hand on his shoulder, and drapes her arm on his shoulder.

Victor wraps his arm around her waist and smiles, and he says, "I will not let go of you."

Then he begins to twirl her in the air, to the excitement of the guests.

The tone of the melody moves from enchanting to haunting. The members of the orchestra, the guests, and the mayor feel that the haunting tone is Carlo's way of accompanying Victor and Julieta's spine-chilling waltz.

But Victor is not fooled by the change in tune. Victor can feel the contempt of Carlo's soul. As a performer, Victor can appreciate someone's disdain for being upstaged. The haunting melody and the indignation in Carlo's eyes are not solely from being upstaged, but also because Victor broke the spell his melody had over Julieta, a melody she inspired in him by her mere presence.

Carlo abruptly stops playing his violin. The music crashes to a stop. Victor stops waltzing, and he holds Julieta two feet above the floor. He tenderly smiles at her. Smiling, she closes her eyes, and then she inhales and exhales. She opens her eyes, and with a nervous smile, she grips his hand and anchors her arm on his shoulder. She looks down between them, and she sees that she is standing in mid-air. She points her toe down and feels nothing. The astounded guests watch as she glides her toe between them on nothing. Victor slowly lowers himself a foot. Julieta's panicked eyes plead with him. Victor whispers, "Trust me."

Julieta slowly lets go of his shoulder, and Victor holds on to her hand as he lands on the marble floor. As Julieta smiles nervously, Victor, looking up at her, kisses her hand and then lets it go.

A loud collective gasp echoes through the ballroom. Julieta is suspended in midair. Her toes are pointing downward like a ballerina's, and the tail of her dress cascades down to the floor.

"With your permission," Victor begs as he places his hands around her waist, and then he slowly glides her down until her feet are firmly on the marble floor.

The uproarious applause is drenched with relief for her safe landing. Julieta does not address the applauding guests; in disbelief, she stares at Victor as he lovingly looks at her.

Carlo yanks his tie off and throws it down on the marble floor.

The guests debate among themselves whether they were treated to a planned performance by Victor in concert with Carlo or an impromptu battle of the egos. What is agreed upon by all is that they were fortunate to be part of whatever just took place.

The enthralled guests fail to see the envy in Carlo's eyes as he walks over to Victor and Julieta. Carlo does not acknowledge Victor's cool eyes. He looks at Julieta. Julieta looks at Victor and Carlo, and she exhales then says, "I am surprised I am still standing."

"You were a vision. Your beauty and poise eclipsed Senor Montenegro's illusion. I still hold hope that you will sing along to my melodies, even if only one."

"Perhaps you should discuss that with Julieta at another time," Victor says decisively.

"Yes, I need to catch my breath," Julieta says, excusing herself.

She walks away at the sound of the guests' applause as Victor and Carlo engage in a cold stare.

Victor looks over at the orchestra, and instantly all the players surround Carlo, raining down on him compliments, questions, and requests.

Victor strides away in search of Julieta. Julieta is sitting on a marble bench in the courtyard. Her lips and face are drained of color. Victor removes his dress jacket and drapes it over her bare shoulders, and then he sits next to her.

"It is a beautiful night," Victor says with a tender smile.

"A mysterious night," Julieta expresses.

"Are you afraid of me?" Victor asks.

"I do not want to be," Julieta stresses.

"Please do not fear me, my dear Julieta," Victor pleads.

"I am captivated by you. I love being in your world of illusions. But your power is so great that it does frighten me at times."

Julieta looks up at Victor's kind and confident eyes. She pushes her arms through the sleeves of his coat, and then she pulls her hair up from underneath the collar, and she observes how Victor watches with tender eyes as her hair falls down on his jacket. She crisscrosses his jacket over her torso.

"I respect you. I recognize all you have done for my family, and I am grateful. I love sharing the stage with you. I do not fear you." Julieta looks away from his smile. "While enchanting, there is a part of me that fears your magic."

"I promise not to ever surprise you with an illusion. I was carried away by the music."

"I know part of the charm is the element of surprise, and I…" Julieta looks away.

"Please, finish what you were going to say," Victor pleads softly.

"After the tour, are we to go our separate ways, or am I…"

Victor interrupts her, "You are free to do what you wish, what will make you and your family happy. You owe me nothing. It is I who owe you the world for your companionship on stage."

Julieta relaxes her arms, and his coat opens. She can feel his warmth reach her heart.

"The stage would be lonely without you," Julieta confesses.

Julieta notices Victor exhaling with gratitude.

"Will we remain partners on the stage?" Julieta asks.

"I wish to be more than your stage partner. I wish to have your trust. I want you to count on me. I want to continue to help your family. I wish to have your esteem."

Juliet stands up and walks away. Victor stands up and watches her patiently as she struggles with the energy between them.

"We do share a bond, Victor. But I am not sure what kind of bond. I fear that I..."

Victor calmly walks to her and takes her hand in his hands, and he says, "I will never expect more than you can give. All I ask is that you forgive me when I am compelled by tenderness for you."

Julieta smiles at Victor, and then she anchors her arm into his.

Carlo finds them standing at the threshold of the foyer, Victor's dress jacket held tightly around her sensual gown, her hair loose over the collar. Victor is standing tall, his feet spread apart, his arm pressing her hand into his torso. They both gallantly smile at the attention from the guests passing by.

As Julieta and Victor turn to each other to comment, Carlo, with a vengeful heart, raises his violin. When Carlo lowers his violin, Victor feels Julieta lose her hold on him, and Victor catches her as she faints. As the guests gasp, Victor lifts her listless body into his arms. Carlo pushes through the worried guests, and as Victor's concerned eyes study her, Carlo gently brushes her hair off her face as he accuses Victor, "You overwhelmed her. Your illusions are draining her. I pray she is all right."

Victor pulls her closer to his chest and yells for Stewart.

"Hand her to me; I'll have my private doctor attend to her," Carlo demands.

"She will be seen by my doctors," Victor declares as he pushes past him, carrying Julieta to the coach as Stewart ushers the guests away to clear a path.

Julieta's condition baffles the most seasoned doctors that money can provide. They all agree that she is still alive but in a state of coma. The mystery to the team of doctors is how she suddenly fainted and fell into this coma state.

Victor refuses to let Julieta's state break him. Victor finds strength in his personal doctor's statement, "As long as she is still among the living, there is hope."

However, in the depths of his soul, Victor knows that it is not hope that will wake her but a miracle.

After hours of his heart tormenting him with the feeling that Julieta is not sleeping, but rather that he is seated next to a living corpse, he tears himself away from her side. In the closed hospital room, standing in the shadows, he stares out into the night, waiting. Against the moon he sees her; he opens the windows, and Suzette flies in. As Suzette retracts her bat wings, Victor takes her hands and showers them kisses.

"Thank you for answering my call."

"Why did you not consult me sooner? I am the oldest living doctor."

"It is not out of lack of confidence in you as a doctor but out of respect for your heart."

Suzette examines the woman Victor is in love with. In a professional tone, she asks, "History of seizures?"

"No."

"Was she suffering from influenza?"

"No."

"Was she in a mental institution?"

"I beg your pardon, Doctor?"

Suzette walks over to Victor and glares at him.

"No. Why do you ask?" Victor answers.

"Medical institutions have a convenient habit of inducing a coma in their patients."

"She was fine. It was a lively evening. She was social and alert. Not even a hint of being tired. We were conversing when she fainted."

Suzette walks back to Julieta's bedside. Without looking at her, she says, "I fear she is not suffering from anything that conventional medicine can address."

"My God! What are you suggesting, Suzette?"

Suzette walks up to Victor and places her palm on the side of his face. "I will do what I can for her," she promises.

Suzette then walks to the open window and says, "I will locate someone who works with energy."

Dark smoke snakes onto the floor from the window. The smoke then morphs into the shape of a woman.

"This is Amy," Suzette says. "Please allow her to examine Julieta."

Victor nods.

Amy takes a couple of steps toward Julieta, and she stops.

"This woman is not ill. Her body is still alive. This is all I can say."

"Break her spell!" Suzette demands.

"I cannot. She is under a dark spell, a spell commissioned by the dark prince, my master."

"He seeks to torment you, my love," Suzette laments.

Victor slams his body against the wall in anger. Blood tears escape Suzette's eyes. "I do not want to see you suffer," she says.

"She needs a miracle. She deserves a miracle," Victor demands.

"I do not do miracles. While I work with black magic, I cannot undo what he has done," Amy declares.

Victor walks up to Suzette, takes hold of her shoulders, and says, "You are a great doctor, but you cannot do anything for her. Amy's magic is powerless against him. I am an illusionist who has fallen out of grace," he laments.

Victor walks away from Suzette and Amy and stands next to Julieta's bedside. "Is this her fate? To languish in this state until her body withers away? This is my fault."

"I will not and cannot help you," Amy says. She twirls into a tunnel of smoke and disappears.

"Well, at least she confirmed my suspicion," Suzette says, frustrated with Amy.

Suzette walks to the window. Victor's shadow grows as his posture freezes with grief.

"Light magic!" Suzette exclaims.

"What?" Victor asks.

Suzette leans out the window, and Victor's coach glides through the shadows and pulls up against the window. Suzette gives Stewart instructions.

The coach departs, and Suzette says to Victor, "It is dark magic that has her under a spell; white magic will break the spell."

An hour later, Victor's coach pulls up at the window.

"She is here, our miracle worker," Suzette says, relieved.

Victor helps the woman climb in through the window.

"I am Lucy. How can I help you?"

"Thank you for coming," Suzette says graciously.

Lucy's rosary beads wrap around one hand, and in her other hand, she holds a small crucifix.

"Please, do not fear. We wish you no harm. We are desperate for your help. I live in the shadows, but I long for the light," Victor pleads as he and Suzette glide away from her. Victor feels his skin burn from the heat emanating from the crucifix. Suzette stands behind Victor and keeps her eyes on Julieta.

Lucy looks at Suzette and Victor with kind eyes. As she slowly scans the room, she puts her fist with the rosary against her heart.

"The darkness overwhelms this room," Lucy says. She then walks over to Julieta's bedside.

Lucy places her hand with the rosary over Julieta's hand, and she is thrust into a trance. With her eyes closed, she reports, "This woman is not ill. Her soul has left her body but not this world. Her soul is in captivity, through no fault of her own, kept by an indentured servant of the dark one."

"Why?" Victor demands.

"Her soul is a muse. I hear beautiful music, and I feel a love racked with desperation."

"Is she in love with someone?" Suzette asks Victor.

"No," Victor answers.

"Is there hope for her?" Suzette asks Lucy.

"She is a child of God; there is hope. She is held against her wish. Once her soul is free, it will return to her body, and she will awaken."

"Where is her soul?" Victor pleads.

"She is an instrument of music," Lucy says.

"She is songstress," Victor corrects.

"She is in an instrument," Lucy clarifies.

"I am afraid I do not follow," Victor says, frustrated.

"She looks out from rows of strings. She is in a string instrument," Lucy says.

"That demon has her!" Victor rages.

Lucy raises her hand off Julieta's hand. She pulls a small vial out of her coat pocket and respectfully holds it out to Victor.

Victor asks, "What is in the vial?"

"It contains holy water and holy oils. Because you wish to rescue her soul, you may therefore take hold of this holy vial without worry."

Victor takes the vial.

Lucy then instructs, "Her soul is in an instrument. Pour the holy water and oils over the instrument, and her soul will rush back to her body. But be warned: if her captor learns that you are coming to release her soul, he will transfer her soul into another vessel. You must employ the element of surprise."

Lucy kisses her rosary and walks back to the window, where she stands under the rays of the moon.

Victor pulls out a purse with gold coins.

"I do not charge for light work," Lucy says.

"Please, take it to help others," Victor pleads.

Lucy takes the purse as the coach pulls up next to the window.

"I apologize for the coach arrangement. We need to be discreet..."

"I understand," Lucy assures Victor.

Victor goes down to the floor on one knee and extends his hand. "Madame," he says, gesturing to Lucy.

Lucy takes his hand and steps onto his thigh, and then Victor's coachman lifts her through the window.

The coach departs, and Victor remains on one knee, recovering from the burning pain.

"I am sure she was very light," Suzette jests as she comes out of the shadows.

"Suzette, please, she is a messenger from God."

"You are right, my love. Forgive me."

Victor stands up and gratefully hugs Suzette. Suzette holds him close, savoring his body close to hers. After a minute, Victor gently pulls away, and he walks to stand next to Julieta. As he contemplates her listless body, his eyes become red with rage.

"A rescue is a plate better served cold. You must have your wits for her sake," Suzette counsels as she walks to him. Her eyes scan his face with medical attunement. "You are lacking iron, and your tone is gray. You must get a feeding. You do not want Julieta to awake and look up to see a living corpse. We have two hours before daybreak. Let us go to the slaughterhouse for fresh blood."

Standing in the line outside of the slaughterhouse overwhelms Suzette. She can hear the people in line silently praying that they will be either cured or spared from the disease that will cause them to cough up their own blood, thus spilling out their life. Suzette and Victor do not exchange words or look at each other. Their demeanor mirrors that of the others in the line, whose postures reveal their fear of the ghastly consumption disease. Everyone respects the somber nature of the line and patiently waits for their turn, as no one wants to be deprived of the life-sustaining blood.

After they drink the slaughter blood, Victor takes leave of Suzette to plan Julieta's rescue. He takes refuge from the warmth of the rising sun in a mausoleum. The mausoleum's ornate stained-glass windows depicting saints ground his fury to kill her captor.

Julieta's Nightmare

Julieta is aware of her existence but not of her surroundings. Music is the oxygen that keeps her alive. In her delirium, images of a man performing magic on a stage comfort her, and the silhouette of a man cradling his violin torments her.

Carlo has not performed for an audience since taking her captive. The melodies his violin performs are jealously kept for his ears only. Every piece of furniture is draped with sheets of music filled with the notes that are sung from his violin. The melodies are heavy with emotions. The melancholy notes weigh on the listener's soul. Carlo feels privileged to be the only audience. While the songs pull at his heart and haunt his soul, he is hopeful that, with time, love will change the tone of the violin's music.

For the time being, Carlo guards his violin, which holds the love of his life. He sleeps only three hours each night because sleep is too much like death. He does not want sleep to keep him away from the company that resides in his violin. His soul demands that his body live the only heaven he will ever have, which is life on earth with his violin holding his true love.

Carlo gently lays the bow against his violin's strings and whispers, "Sing to me, my love."

Julieta's soul is compelled by his command. Her feelings brought on by the broken stream of flashbacks set the tone.

Carlo waits to feel her vibration of the strings of the violin against his bow as a sign to start interpreting her melodies.

The state of her soul, imprisoned in his violin, and his soul, imprisoned in an evil contract, encourages creativity, the only freedom in the room, to soar to heights that their former free selves could only dream of.

Each song that the violin sounds from her soul is unique. Carlo does not allow himself to think that his private concerts are commissioned by evil. The melodies that he and she create through his violin are the most beautiful songs his professional ears have ever had the privilege of hearing. And as he captures the notes on music sheets, he thinks about how audiences will be moved by the emotional songs.

Victor bursts through the French doors of Carlo's balcony.

"Must you be so dramatic? Can't you use the bedroom door like a civilized human being?" Carlo mocks.

Carlo sits on an overstuffed chair pulled up next to his desk, which is illuminated by candles, holding his violin against his chest.

Victor's enraged eyes survey Carlo's bedroom, taking in the music sheets filled with notes that cover the surfaces like confetti.

"Release her!" Victor demands.

Carlo looks at the music sheet on his desk and assures him, "I will release each and every one of these beautiful songs."

"Release Julieta's soul at once, or I will release your soul and send it crashing down to the pit of hell."

"Interesting threat from someone who is as condemned as me," Carlo says as he shifts nervously in his comfortable chair, clutching his violin to his chest.

"I am not going to argue with a man who sold his soul to the devil."

Victor walks up to him and hovers over him, his eyes an enraged red. Victor pulls out a dagger. As he is about to stab Carlo in the heart, from the corner of his eyes he sees two ghastly things spring up from the floorboards. The gruesome creatures are not there to protect Carlo but to encourage Victor's evil act.

Carlo winces at the sight of the things, with their hideous black eyes illuminated by fire, and he hugs the violin.

Victor throws his dagger into the air, and it vanishes. He pulls the vial of holy water from his jacket's breast pocket and removes the cork. He throws the holy water and holy oils onto the violin. Carlo suffers burns from the holy water and holy oils. Splashed with drops of the holy water and holy oils, the diabolical things groan with utter pain as they dive back down through the floorboards. A white mist escapes the violin, and Julieta's spirit flows through Victor and out of the French balcony doors he crashed through.

"You come near her again, and I will grant the devil fast delivery of you!" Victor says as he employs his bat wings and flies out through the French doors.

Carlo is heartbroken by the departure of Julieta's spirit. He lets the violin, now cold and lifeless, drop to the floor. Carlo ignores the pain of his burns as he picks up the last music sheet he was working on. The notes slowly lift from the page and vanish into the air. Carlo stands up in a panic. He reaches for another sheet just in time to see the notes lift off and also vanish. As he is about to reach for another sheet, he notices that the air around him is sprinkled with notes written by his hand, dictated to him by Julieta's soul. As the notes continue to vanish from the air, Carlo opens a drawer and pulls out clean music sheets. Pen in hand, he is ready to capture the notes that are escaping. As he puts pen to paper, his hand becomes paralyzed.

Carlo feels the weight of his curse. He throws the pen and collapses on the floor, surrounded by music sheets devoid of notes. In a panic, he reaches for his violin. From memory, he tries to play the last melody they created, but he cannot recall the notes. He finds he has no memory of any of the music that they created in the last three days. He slams his violin to the floor. Julieta's spirit is gone. Her musical notes have vanished; his memory cannot recollect her melodies. All that he has of those three days with her spirit is the memory of the euphoria of holding her close.

Victor rushes into the hospital room and finds Julieta standing with the help of a nurse. Victor takes a moment to catch his breath, and he gently approaches her. She gives him a smile. Relieved, Victor embraces her as he says, "You had me so worried. I thought I lost you."

"What happened to me?" Julieta asks.

"You fell into a coma," Victor says.

"If it were not for Mr. Montenegro, you would have been buried alive. Your vital signs were too low to detect," the nurse informs Julieta.

A ghastly color replaces the faint pink of her cheeks as Julieta sits herself down on the visitor's chair.

"The last thing I remember is standing at your side at the gala," Julieta says as the frown in her forehead deepens.

As the nurse tidies up the room, she says, "Mr. Montenegro saw to it that you were cared for by the best doctors in town as you wallowed in a deep sleep for several days."

"I am plagued with nightmarish memories of constantly having to hear and play music as if I were an instrument," Julieta says.

The nurse pours water into a glass and then hands it to Julieta as she says, "Perhaps what did you in was stage fatigue."

Julieta shakes her head, and holding the full glass of water, she looks up to Victor and says, "It is not stage fatigue. There is no other place in the world where I feel more alive than on the stage. Besides, I am a singer, not a composer. And yet in my head, I have faint recollections of songs that I never heard before I fell into the coma, yet the songs feel as personal to me as my soul."

"I, for one, am looking forward to getting you back to your family and back on the stage," Victor beams.

Julieta's cracked and dry lips smile at him before she takes a sip of water.

Tears of rancor salt the burns on his face as he trembles with defeat. The light of his life was rescued from his musical prison. The music they created together evaporated like a dream. With clenched teeth, he struggles with his stupidity for not wishing to keep her forever.

"You are a musical genius, but your stupidity is staggering," says the dark thing, dressed in fine clothes.

"Let me be," Carlo begs.

"I am not God. You do not have free will with me. What you do have is a contract. A contract that you will uphold. You had your wish; you lived with her spirit for several days. Now, you must perform as the master commands."

"I do not have the will," Carlo pleads.

"That is right. You do not have will. With no free will, you will do as ordered."

Carlo picks up his violin and looks at it, and then he cries, "This no longer has value for me, not without her."

An unseen punch hits him. The blow throws him to the floor, and he lands on his violin.

As the thing stares at the wall, Carlo picks himself up and lifts the damaged violin, gazing at the broken instrument.

A new violin materializes on the seat from which he was thrown.

Carlo drops his damaged violin and picks up the new violin. He asks, "An enchanted violin?"

"No. Nothing peculiar about the violin. You are the enchanted instrument. You had your wish with her. Now get back to work."

"It is impossible to think that I can create music like the music she and I created."

"Is that what you desire to create? The tortured music of a captive soul?"

"I am tortured and captive, but she possesses an element that gave depth to the music that I fear I will never have."

"Freedom," the thing says as he growls with laughter.

Profound sadness clothes Carlo's face. The thing responses to his sadness with mocking laughter.

Carlo looks up and stares into the thing's frightening eyes, and he declares, "I may not have freedom, but I still have wishes per my contract."

"Two wishes remaining," the demon says.

"I want the music that she and I created returned to me."

The music notes begin to rain down from the ceiling onto the blank sheets scattered about the room.

Carlo springs up from his chair, and as he collects the sheets, now filled with music notes, he smiles at each sheet as the music is played in head.

The thing cuts into his euphoric thoughts and asks him, "What will you say to Julieta when she asks about your sudden disfigurement?"

Carlo continues to collect his beloved music sheets as the smile on his face drops.

"I must say, your audience will be too distracted by your pitiful facial burns to really appreciate the music that Julieta and, of course, you created."

Carlo presses the music sheets against his chest as he sits back down.

"You have one wish remaining," the demons suggests.

A gilded mirror appears in midair in front of Carlo. Carlo slowly looks at his image in the mirror. The holy water and holy oils seared three deep slashes stretching from his forehead to across his nose and lips and down to his neck.

"Can these burns be removed?" Carlo asks.

"No. It is the new you. Each and every time you see your image, the burns will be there. Trace your fingers over the burns, and you will feel the scars. However, if you so wish, the scars will only be visible to your eyes, and only your fingers will be able to feel them," the demon says.

Carlo looks back at the mirror; instead of his image, he sees Julieta's unscathed face. Julieta's lovely face fades, and the mirror plays images of people on the streets, in cafés, and at concerts reacting to Carlo's burns with horror and suspicion in their eyes. In the last image, he watches as Julieta recoils in terror as his burns bring back memories of her imprisonment at his hands.

"I wish that my burns are not visible to anyone on this planet," Carlo utters.

"No one but you," the demon corrects.

Carlo solemnly nods.

"Your last wish is granted. His darkness has honored the contract. You must also honor the contract. Get back to work and perform."

Julieta embraces the doctors' diagnosis of a coma brought on by exhaustion due to her tour. To avoid fearing for her sanity, Julieta clings to the doctors' explanation that people in comas have vivid and surreal dreams to explain her memories of being held captive.

Julieta pulls Victor in for a grateful hug. She thanks him for taking care of her and not worrying her family. Still clinging to him, she pleads, "For days I lay as if I were dead. I want to live, and nowhere do I feel more alive than on stage with the grand illusionist Victor Montenegro."

Julieta slowly pulls away from his arms and searches his eyes for agreement. Victor smiles; he knows that her state was not brought on by exhaustion and that she is fit to perform. "We shall perform tomorrow night!" he says.

Victor escorts Julieta to the St. Francis Hotel. Victor suggests that she should spend the evening having a good meal, and he orders her to take advantage of room service to pamper herself and enjoy being back in her suite, made homey by the many family photos and all her personal belongings. Victor takes a moment to contemplate her as she stands in the middle of the room, her face flush with color and smiling, grateful to be back in her suite.

"Will you dine with me?" Julieta asks.

"I would love to, but I have an international meeting. Besides, I feel you should have time to yourself to indulge and have a proper rest."

Julieta nods.

Victor walks up to her and kisses her hand. "I cannot find the words to express how grateful and relieved I am to see you well and out of the hospital," he says.

"Thank you for all your care," Julieta says warmly.

"Good night, Julieta. I will call on you at dusk tomorrow night. If you need anything at any time, I pray you will contact me."
"Yes, thank you. Good night, Victor."

Victor does not have an international meeting. He got wind that Carlo was performing, and Victor felt compelled to see him perform. Victor has many questions about Carlo's involvement with darkness and what power he holds that enabled him to imprison Julieta.

Carlo's concert is an intimate gathering in the ballroom of a private residence. Victor, cloaked and with his hat snugly low on his head, appears in the shadow of a seven-foot marble statue at the back of the audience. In attendance are a hundred or so prominent people. Victor notices that there is no trace of the burns inflicted on Carlo's face from the holy water and holy oils that splashed him when Victor doused the violin in his arms.

Carlo begins to play a new melody Victor has never heard. The emotional notes of the serene melody vibrate in Victor's heart. Victor is astounded by how deeply the melody of his nemesis affects him emotionally, as if the melody is crying out to him. The captivated audience is moved. Victor notices how the ladies step back from the stage as they press their handkerchiefs under their eyes. The gentlemen straighten their posture as they glue their eyes on Carlo's violin. The next melody again creates an emotional response from Victor. He is sure he has never heard that melody before, yet it moves him with such familiarity that it frightens him. Victor focuses his attention on Carlo's forehead, and Victor is struck with images of Carlo's inspiration for the melodies. In Carlo's energy, Victor can see his violin interpreting Julieta's emotions into music and Carlo writing down the notes. Victor opens his palm, revealing a ball of raging fire. He looks at the ball of overlapping flames, and just before he is about to strike Carlo with it, he gets the image of the vial of holy water and holy oils that released Julieta from her devilish prison. With a clap, he extinguishes the ball of fire in his palm, and he opens his hands to unleash a cloud of smoke. The members of the audience, coughing violently, exit the ballroom. The smoke clears from the empty ballroom. Carlo searches through the sea of candlelight and smoke for a clue as to what is going on. Victor pulls back his cloak and removes his hat. Carlo hears Victor's dress shoes against the wooden floor as Victor approaches the stage.

"Out of pity for your wretched soul, I will spare your life. I will spare your life just this one time. Keep your distance from Julieta. If you harm her again, I will personally walk you to the gates of hell."

Victor puts his hat back on, and then he disappears. As Carlo tries to recover from the fear of almost being dispatched to hell, his ears are assaulted by guttural laughter. Carlo, in agony, covers his head with his hands and pleads, "Please, stop."

The laughter ceases. A well-dressed man appears in a pool of fire, and he says to Carlo, "Carlo Fini, love is not in the cards. Señor Montenegro is gravely serious about his threat to see you dead and in hell. But it is not your time. Hell will be there for an eternity. You are needed among the living. Your rags-to-riches story has inspired many to have a pact with the devil. You must honor your contract, or you will suffer the torture that is reserved for hell on earth."

The demon disappears, leaving behind the scent of death in the hot and smoky ballroom. The owner of the house runs in, grabs Carlo by the arm, and escorts him out of the bad air of the ballroom.

After an enjoyable tea with women of high society who had pledged money to the hospital that nursed her back to health, Julieta rushes to her suite to rest, after which she will meet Victor for an early dinner before the evening show.

She opens the double doors to her suite, and her bright room, decorated in hues of white and gold, is filled with orange roses in every direction she looks. She walks to the biggest bouquet, which holds thirty orange roses, and takes the card nestled against the thorns. The card reads, "My lady, it fills me with gratitude and joy to hear you are well and performing again. My tour in San Francisco has come to an end. I will return to our beloved city, Montenegro, in the morning. You are an inspiration. I look forward to hearing you sing again. With esteem, Carlo Fini."

The card slips out of her hand and falls to the floor. A wave of panic smothers her. As she scans the roses in her suite, an overwhelming sense of fear and nausea storms inside her. She exits her suite and stands in the hallway, composing herself and calming her spirit.

"Are you all right, Madame?"

Julieta looks up. Standing in front of her is the bellboy, holding a large bouquet of fresh roses that Victor has ordered to warm her suite.

Julieta opens her arms to receive the bouquet. The bellboy carefully hands her the bouquet of fresh roses of every color but orange. As Julieta hugs the bouquet, she pleads, "Please have all the bouquets currently in my suite removed immediately."

In the hallway, Julieta watches the parade of roses exiting her suite. The bellboy looks at the bouquet in her arms and asks, "Madame, should I take this bouquet as well, or should I place it on the table in your suite?"

Julieta holds the bouquet closer and says, "I will take care of this bouquet."

Victor, on his way to his suite, which is across from Julieta's suite, arrives in the hallway and walks past the train of hotel personnel carrying away the bouquets of orange roses. Victor lowers his head to hide his grin at the rejection of the bouquets. Victor looks up and sees Julieta in front of her suite doors, holding his bouquet, watching the last of Carlo's rejected bouquets turn the corner.

"Are roses no longer your favorite?" Victor asks Julieta.

Julieta looks at the bouquet of roses in her arms. She tenderly smiles at them, and then she responds, "They are still my favorite, but those roses made me ill."

"Ill?"

"Yes, they are farewell roses from Mr. Carlo Fini."

"Farewell?"

"Yes, he returns to Montenegro in the morning."

"Does his departure sadden you?" Victor asks.

"It is peculiar…the mere mention of his name upsets me," Julieta confesses with a confused expression.

"I do not care for Fini. I do not feel I can trust him professionally, which makes me question whether I can trust him personally," Victor says.

Julieta smiles as her shoulders relax.

"Permit me," Victor says as he takes the bouquet from her arms. As he relishes the warmth from her body hugging the vase, he slowly walks to the grand circular table in the foyer and places the bouquet on the shiny table.

"Thank you," Julieta says as she looks around her suite, now cleared of any trace of Carlo.

Victor takes Julieta's hand, but instead of grasping her bent hand, he lifts the back of her left hand and kisses her open palm.

Julieta does not retract her hand. Julieta looks into his sensual gray eyes, which penetrate her eyes, and she confesses, "There are moments that I feel that the same energy that surrounds Fini also surrounds you."

Victor holds on to her gaze. She adds, "While I do not understand the mystery of Victor Montenegro, in my heart, I feel that I can trust you."

Victor warmly smiles and says, "It is my hope that you never cease to trust me. I am at your command, and I will obey your rules."

Julieta, smiling, nods.

"I'll leave you so you can rest. I will call in a couple of hours," Victor says, and then he lifts both of her hands to his lips and kisses each one before he departs.

Carlo looks at his image in the mirror. He stares at the burns on his face that no one else but him can see. The deep burns across his face are a constant reminder of the fate that awaits his soul. He traces the burns with his finger, and he finds comfort in the mounds of scars etched in him by the hand of God: his dark contract and his caprice to attain global musical dominance have not completely cut him off from God. He looks at the three scars across his face and says out loud, "The Father, the Son, and the Holy Spirit."

The pangs of regret for contracting with darkness and his despair to be free from the clutches of the devil gnaw at him.

Carlo thinks about his love for Julieta. He thinks about Victor's presence in Julieta's life, and he feels envious. His mad love for her pushed his desperation to imprison her soul in his violin. Carlo pulls the small mirror off the wall and sits down on a chair illuminated by the sun streaming in through the window. He holds the mirror up and stares at the three scars across his face, longing to go back in time. Instead of signing the devil's contract with his blood, he wishes he would have spit on it and walked away.

He stares at the scars on his face as he thinks about God's immense love for and command over his whole creation. Deep sadness and lament grip him as he wonders what his life would have been if he had never been seduced by the devil. The image of him in the mirror freezes. Carlo moves his head, but his image is as still as a painting. As Carlo stares at his lifeless image, the scars expand and begin to burn with lakes of fire. Horrified, Carlo cannot pull himself away from the sight. The mirror begins to feel hot, and Carlo drops the mirror to the floor, where it breaks into three large pieces. Dark smoke snakes up from the cracked and hot mirror. Carlo watches as the black smoke takes shape in the form of a hideous demon. The red eyes of the hideous reptilian demon glare at Carlo. Carlo presses himself against the back of his padded chair to get away from the smell of rotten flesh exuding from the demon.

"Your fate is sealed. A change of heart will not erase the sin from the book of life. Your soul is no longer yours to barter with."

The demon's red eyes look at the fine padded chair Carlo's body is pressed against, and it says, "Honor your contract so you may still enjoy the comfort of your chair, or suffer torment."

The demon punches his claw into the black smoke he is levitating on and pulls out Carlo's violin, which he places on Carlo's lap, "Your violin is tuned. Get to work."

The smoke and the demon are sucked back through the cracked mirror and into hell, leaving behind the stench of rotten flesh.

Carlo stands up, puts the violin on the chair, and jumps over the cracked mirror that the demon crawled out of. He runs out the door.

Carlo sits in his courtyard, surrounded by the sweet smell of flowers. He observes as birds escape the noon sun by flying to the shaded tree branches. The breeze that gently caresses the leaves and flower petals lifts the smell of rotten flesh clinging to his garments up to his nose.

Carlo, sitting on the marble water fountain's bench, rocks back and forth. Carlo turns toward the sound of the birds splashing in the water fountain, and he looks at his image in the water. His scars, still seeping lava, taunt his soul. Carlo wishes his torment was insanity and not the taunts of the devil.

He looks away, and he trembles underneath the noon sun. Despair and desperation claw at his soul as his heart fills with dread at the thought of an eternity in hell. His enchanted violin, now perched on the windowsill, beckons him to come inside and compose. Carlo can feel his violin against the window; he can feel eyes from hell watching him.

Despite his lack of privacy due to his hellish watchers, his mind runs wild, searching for an escape. The burning sensation from his scars breaks into his thoughts, and he thinks about the contents of the vial that rescued Julieta. Images of churches, saints, and Jesus run through his mind, and he thinks about divine forgiveness and intervention. He knows that the things that shadow him will prevent him from entering a church, and he expects mental, physical, and emotional torment if he takes it upon himself to pray for salvation. He feels that his only chance is for someone to intervene for him and pray for his soul. He will plead with Montenegro for the name of the light worker who helped to free Julieta. An eruption blasts through the stone ground of his courtyard, and through it rises the devil himself. He steps out of the dark hole, and the ground shakes under his hooved feet. The beast's head blocks the sun; each of his two horns stretches six feet long. The beast's eyes, lakes of fire filled with tormented souls, burn through Carlo. The beast's clawed hand wraps around Carlo's neck, raises him up to his immense head, and then shakes him. Carlo, petrified, chokes on the beast's foul snorts, which reek of burning and rotten flesh.

"How dare you even think you can conspire to null your contract with me? You pathetic fool! I own you. You've forfeit the small peace that was afforded to you outside of the gates of hell."

The devil's clawlike nail slashes across Carlo's throat. The devil dumps Carlo's body into the fountain. The devil spits a butcher knife into the fountain, and the knife plants itself next to Carlo's hand.

The devil's guttural laughter booms in his ears as Carlo stares at his lifeless body at the bottom of the fountain. As blood from his slashed throat rises to the surface of the water, four demons take hold of his wretched soul. The four demons claw and bite his soul as they all tumble together down the hole into hell.

The next day, Carlo's housekeeper enters his music room. She does not find Carlo. She looks at the violin perched on the windowsill. The sight of the violin standing on its own accord sends chills through the housekeeper, and she runs from the property, screaming for the neighbors.

The neighbors soon find Carlo's body and pull it from the fountain. One neighbor points at his slashed throat. Using a rake, the neighbors blindly comb the bottom of the fountain, obscured by the bloody water, and drag up the knife.

Carlo Fini's death is ruled a suicide. Those close to him speak of Carlo as being a tormented genius who could no longer live in this world that was too small for his music. Others argue that his genius was sanctioned by darkness, and he could no longer live as a fraud. What all could agree on was that his soul would not rest in peace.

In hell, Carlo's torture is not without an audience. As he suffers the fires of hell, he is forced to drink boiling water, and his spiritual being suffers the wounds and pain that will kill flesh and blood, but he is forced to live through the pain over and over. Carlo is coerced to hold concerts until his hands bleed while being tormented by demons as they mock him as the greatest tortured violinist in hell.

The reports of the great Carlo Fini playing haunting melodies at his gravesite are too numerous to be ignored. For those who behold the vision, it is a moving sight of the ghost of the once revered musician sitting atop the headstone that bears his name. He is playing enchanting music, away from hell and within the beautiful world where he desperately wants to remain. For those three hours, he gladly plays the most beautiful melodies to earn his furlough from hell so that he can feel the midnight breeze and the coolness of his marble grave under an illuminating moon.

Thus, Carlo continues to work for the devil. When the moon coasts over his gravesite at midnight, Carlo's spirit, with his violin in his shadowy hands, sits on his marble slab and plays his haunting melodies until three in the morning. Musicians flock to his gravesite in these hours to hear his unearthly music. Some musicians are rendered insane in their attempt to capture the notes so they can play them. Other musicians are seduced by the eerie, unholy, yet elegant melodies into signing contracts with the devil so they can play the songs only heard by their ears. Thousands pay to hear the newly contracted musicians play the melodies that were written in hell, and those in the audience, as they make the sign of the cross, marvel at how such beautiful music can be produced in the worst place in God's creation. The musicians who are not rendered insane by the moving melodies or haven't made a pact with the devil are nightly haunted by the melodies, which entice them to return to Carlo's gravesite to sign a contract.

The news of Fini's death is welcomed by Victor, but it also serves as a warning. Being in love with the same woman was not the only thing in common between Victor and the late Carlo. They both shared the same desperate resolve to stay away from the gates of hell. Carlo failed in his resolve, and Victor takes heed. Victor can feel it in his bones that Carlo did not commit suicide but was dragged to hell by Satan himself. Victor felt in Carlo the same desperation to part with darkness for the sake of love, Julieta's love. And it was that desperation to part with darkness that sealed Carlo in hell. Victor's feelings toward Satan consist of both contempt and regard. Victor's hand is stronger than Carlo's was because Victor did not seek out a pact with the devil, and that gives him the leverage to fight for his soul's salvation.

Julieta feels a euphoric freedom wash over her when she hears of Carlo's death. It baffles her that Carlo invokes feelings in her that she cannot reconcile. Inspired by her feeling of freedom, her singing soars, to the pleasure of her audiences and Victor.

April 18, 1906

Julieta's joy for life keeps sleep at bay. One of her wishes came true before midnight when Victor surprised her with tickets to see the living legend Enrico Caruso sing *Carmen* at the Grand Opera House on Mission Street. At the Opera House, Enrico Caruso spotted Victor and Julieta in one of the balconies, and to the delight of the audience, Enrico invited Julieta onto the stage, where she and Enrico sang a duet together. After the opera, Victor and Julieta attended two parties as honorary guests.

Julieta, still trembling with excitement, holds tightly to Victor's arm as he escorts her to her suite at the St. Francis. As they walk down the hall toward their suites, Victor jests, "We will arrive at your door before sunrise, my lady."

"I am still so excited—I hope I can sleep," Julieta says, smiling.

Victor abruptly halts his steps. Julieta recovers her balance from almost tripping from Victor's sudden halt, and she looks at him questioningly.

Victor does not say a word. Julieta can feel that Victor is listening to something she cannot hear.

Victor wraps his arm around her and pulls her close as he stresses, "We must leave the hotel—"

Before he can utter the word *now*, a mighty thrust tears her away, and they are flung in opposite directions. Victor slams against the wall with such force that it leaves a dent nearly the size of his body. Julieta is lifted up, and she lands on her side and clings to an oriental rug in terror. As Victor is about to go to her to help her up, he halts and raises his hand as he has done hundreds of times on stage. Julieta looks up to see a solid wood armoire bowing over her in midair. Frozen in fear and unable to get her balance, she clings to the rug while staring at Victor's commanding hand. While the hotel rocks like a battered ship in a hurricane, Victor's commanding hand holds the eight-foot armoire in the air as crumbling plaster rains down on them and huge paintings crash to the floor amid the sound of shattering glass and porcelain and nightmarish cries from the guest. The rocking stops, and Victor's commanding hand gently lowers the armoire to rest on its side. He then quickly lifts Julieta to her feet and asks her, "Are you all right?"

"That was not an illusion," Julieta says.

"I am afraid not. That was an earthquake," Victor says.

"How on earth were you able to hold up that armoire?" Julieta asks with fear in her tone.

Before Victor can answer, a stronger tremor shakes the floor. Victor's hand commands two locked doors to open, and he holds Julieta in his arms under the door frame. Julieta clings tightly to Victor's dress jacket, praying she will see her family again.

After the twenty-five seconds of horrific rocking comes to an abrupt end, Victor takes a firm hold on her hand and escorts her out of the battered but still standing hotel.

As they walk out into Union Square, the rising sun filters through a cloud of dust hovering over the heart-wrenching devastation. As far as their eyes can scan are battered and crumbling buildings. People scantily dressed, distraught, and in a shocked panic rush to take shelter in the open air. Amid the chorus of wrenching screams, cries of disbelief, moans, and prayers, Julieta and Victor, covered in gray dust, take in the devastation. In every direction, they see structures once mighty in height now collapsed and in heaps. The defaced facades of the buildings that still stand crumble onto the dazed people below. As hundreds of people seek cover under the morning sky in Union Square, mothers hysterically yell out for their missing young. The wailing of those discovering their dead ones in the rubble pierces through the rattles of the aftershocks of the golden city, now in ruins.

Victor turns to the shaking and emotional Juliet. Grasping her arms, he looks into her frightened eyes and then gently and firmly says, "I pray to God that Stewart is still alive for him to see you home. If he is not still with us, I will hire another coach to take you back to Montenegro. I will send word to my brother to send builders and carpenters to help with the cleanup and rebuilding of this great city. I will also request provisions, tents, medicine, and food for those in need. I will also ask my brother to give you money so that you can replace your wardrobe and commission new gowns so that you can return to performing when you are ready."

A tear cuts through the dust on her cheek left by the devastation as she looks up into Victor's eyes and says, "I cannot fathom how you commanded an armoire not to come crashing down on me. Did I dream it? Is this a nightmare?"

Victor pulls her into an embrace, holds her close to steady her shaking, and says, "You will be safe in Montenegro."

"No. I do not want to abandon San Francisco and her people. This community has given me my stardom as a singer, and I must give back and help, even if it is one brick at a time."

Victor and Julieta, worrying about the structural integrity of the St. Francis Hotel, accept the invitation to stay at Mayor Schimtz's resident. The mayor informs Victor that all telephone lines have stopped working. Victor sends word to his brother with a telegram.

As San Franciscans suffer, the rest of the country is summoned by the cries of paperboys holding up their papers, whose devastating headlines proclaim that a monster earthquake has left San Francisco in ruins, with thousands of bodies buried under mountains of rubble. A major aftershock struck at 8:14 in the morning, the papers note, causing numerous damaged buildings to collapse, claiming more souls and furthering the destruction.

In Mayor Schimtz's backyard, Victor reunites with the anxious Julieta, who is relieved to see that Victor has returned unhurt, bringing Stewart with him. To Stewart's surprise, Julieta rushes to Victor's welcoming arms and gratefully hugs him. Julieta releases Victor and hugs Stewart. She pulls back and looks at them and smiles. As tears roll down her face, she says, "Thank God you both are back."

"My dear, I still insist that you return to Montenegro with Stewart. Surely by now your father is extremely worried."

"No, I need to be here. I must help the survivors."

Mayor Schimtz joins them in the backyard. Victor informs him that he sent word to his brother via telegraph to send men, tents, provisions, and food.

"On behalf of all San Francisco citizens, we thank you, Mr. Montenegro. We welcome all the support in our devastating time of need."

Ernesto Montenegro is not in Montenegro. His acting mayor receives Victor's telegraph and immediately begins to gather men and all the necessary supplies to send to San Francisco.

Ernesto Montenegro is in Los Angeles attending a diplomatic meeting. The meeting ends just before noon, and Ernesto, curious about the thousands of people gathering around the bulletin boards, begins walking toward the crowd when the first of two earthquakes strikes; the second hits ten minutes later. The thousands of people run in terror. Ernesto steadies himself on the pulsating ground and then makes his way to the bulletin boards. As the ground continues to shake under his feet, he reads the latest telegraphic dispatches posted on the board about the devastation in San Francisco. A dignitary meets the shocked Ernesto at the bulletin boards and shares that at 10:05 in the morning, the Deforest Wireless Telegraph station in San Diego radioed the USS *Chicago* about the San Francisco disaster, and the USS *Chicago* is now headed full speed toward San Francisco. The dignitary also shared with Ernesto that at 10:30 in the morning, the USS *Preble* from Mare Island landed a hospital shore party on Howard Street.

Ernesto thanks the dignitary and departs to Montenegro to gather aid for San Francisco.

The aftershocks continue without mercy. With every aftershock, Julieta becomes more desperate to help.

"My world in Montenegro is whole and sound. My father and brother are alive and well. We have our lives. My intimate possessions are locked in the hotel, which continues to stand. All around me are the cries of people who have lost everything. I am surrounded by utter devastation and inconsolable suffering. People are paralyzed with so much devastation and suffering; they need people like us who have not lost everything to help them not lose themselves in the ruins," Julieta says as she paces over the cracked dirt that continues to shift under her feet.

"There is no way of knowing when the aftershocks will stop," Stewart says as he sketches images of the devastation that are seared in his mind.

"I know that art is to you what singing is to me. And forgive me for saying this, but I find it unsettling that you sketch the devastation," Julieta says as she wraps her shawl tighter around her.

"I am not trying to capture the suffering. I am trying to record the landscape for historical reference. The ruins must speak to future architects so that structures are designed to better withstand earthquakes. I do not have a family, the room I rent is still standing, and my paintings are safe. The sketches help me to calm my nerves, and hopefully they will serve a purpose. But like you, I am anxious to help," Stewart says, looking at Victor.

Victor walks over to Julieta and says, "I gave my word to your father that I would keep you safe. Your little brother lost his mother; I do not want him to lose you too."

Julieta presses her palm against her forehead. Victor takes her hand away from her forehead and kisses it.

"I do not want to lose you."

The passion in his statement causes Stewart to stop sketching and look over to them.

Julieta steps back, points toward the closed backyard gate, and says, "I am going out there and help,"

"Help how?" Victor gently asks.

Julieta paces and proclaims, "Help a mother locate her lost child. Help the wounded. Help the mayor organize the bread lines. I need to help. I must help."

Stewart puts away his sketches and says, "Mr. Montenegro will be helping the mayor with regaining order in the city and communicating to the world the need for aid. I can team up with you, Lady Julieta, and together we can see what is needed."

"I have reached out to people throughout the world. Help will be arriving from many locations. The mayor is well equipped and staffed—I would just get in his way. I feel it is essential for our safety that we stay together. I will accompany you two."

The trio steps out of the open-air sanctuary and into unfathomable destruction. In every direction, against a gray sky, they see houses that were blasted to the ground and others sunken into the ground. The air is choked with dust and smoke; people walk aimlessly, carrying bundles over their shoulders, dragging trunks over the warped ground. A woman walks past them carrying a birdcage with three kittens inside. As the mothers carry their belongings, wide-eyed and expressionless children cling to their skirts. The cries for help are heard half a block away. People are still trapped under bricks, masonry rendered into dust, and collapsed houses.

Victor and Stewart plunge into the task of unburying the living, while Julieta consoles their loved ones and passes out fruit and slices of bread, given to her by the mayor, to the children.

Inferno

The cry of "Fire!" is heard over and over through the crackling sounds of the infernos and agonizing cries. The firefighters turn in each direction and see that the wreckage all around them is burning. The intense fires melt granite and fan out the scent of burning bodies. Half of the firemen are assigned to fight the fires, while the other half are to rescue people. The firemen fight passionately against the infernos and make heroic efforts to rescue people, but with fifty fires blazing and thousands who need rescuing, the small company of firefighters is overwhelmed.

The earthquake and unmerciful aftershock tremors rolling through the city, famous for the gold rush and the rise of vigilantes, kill thousands. The fires spread, devouring the living who are buried under the collapsed city. Victor and Julieta hear the wrenching cries of a man trapped in the path of the fast-approaching fire. The poor soul begs his rescuers, who are furiously working against the heat and choking smoke to unbury him, to kill him because he does not want to be burned alive. As Victor runs toward the man to help, another man approaches the trapped and pleading man. The man and the trapped man have a short conversation, and just as Victor gets close, the man pulls out his revolver and shoots the trapped man dead to spare him from being burned alive. Victor stops and composes himself as Julieta catches up to him, with tears cascading over the soot on her cheeks.

The firefighting water quickly dries up, and the fires rage on as rivers of thousands of people carrying what they can stream through the catastrophe, seeking a safe place. Many find refuge in the city's parks; others stop in the cemeteries. All attention is on containing the fires and rescuing the living, so the unburied dead are left unattended. Many of the living have no other choice but to sleep between the bodies of the dead and the carcasses of horses that were killed by the earthquake or a humane hand. As Victor walks the streets, rescuing people and helping the firefighters, his overwhelmed spirit is lifted by the coping humor displayed by the survivors. In parks and in cemeteries, Victor comes across signs that declare "Camp Thankful," "Camp Grateful," "Camp Living," and the like.

A new fire ignites when a citizen tries to cook ham and eggs on a stove with a destroyed chimney. This small fire becomes the monster fire that rages on for twenty-four hours, devouring thirty city blocks.

With their city in ruins and the inferno reducing the sea of devastation to ash, the citizens are left to pick up the pieces of their lives from among the rubble and the decaying dead. Their priorities are to find a patch of land that is not cracked or in the path of the fires so that they can rest and have the luxury to think. A few wretched souls seek to capitalize on the city's misfortune by burglarizing wrecked stores and vacant homes and breaking into saloons and stealing liquor. The body of a wealthy woman is discovered with her fingers amputated by a thief in order to steal her expensive rings.

The mayor issues an order to Chief Dinan under the law of necessity that states, "As it has come to my attention that thieves are taking advantage of the present deplorable conditions and are plying their nefarious vocations among the ruins in our city, all peace officers are ordered to instantly kill anyone caught looting or committing any other serious crimes." Many are shot on sight and left to be consumed by the fires. Most of those shot are guilty, but others are not. Victor witnesses a man shot by a soldier for carrying his own chicken. The true treasure that everyone scavenges for under bricks, wood, and stones, while risking being shot, is canned food.

Communicating to the rest of the world the dire need for food is slow and difficult, so to ward off famine, Victor uses telepathy to reach out to his fellow night creatures and implores them to exercise their political connections to stress to the world the monumental need for food. Within a day, shipments of food start arriving from nearby cities, and more bread lines sprout throughout the city, where the homeless and hungry wait in line for food. Police officers seize the food from all grocery stores that are in danger of catching fire, and they deliver the food to the refugees.

Street kitchens emerge throughout the city. People cook their meager meals in the middle of the streets, away from structures, to prevent another ham-and-eggs fire. People share their meals, and they serve humor with the food, with signs that read, "Eat here, but go home to die," "Burnt free food," "Bread without water," "Earthquake shakes—ten cents," and "Café Sinkam," a reference to the popular Café Zinkand.

San Francisco continues to burn. The homeless camping in graveyards gratefully shelter in the vaults for the dead and sorrowfully stare out at the enormous flames devouring the city. The thick smoke of the fires turns the days into nights, affording Victor the ability to help during the days. For three days and three nights, the city burns and crumbles. A fellow vampire hidden in the smoke informs Victor that his brother has loaded wagons and trains with food, medicine, tents, and men and that they are on their way up to San Francisco.

Julieta does not listen to Victor's pleas for her to take a break from the heart-wrenching devastation; in her waking hours, she lives to help others. Victor and Julieta manage to sleep for a few hours at a time.

The inferno rages on, drying up the city's water. The monster fire reaches Van Ness Avenue. Colonel Charles Morris of the Artillery Corps orders the mansions along the street dynamited in a desperate attempt to build a firebreak. The mayor, Victor, Julieta, Stewart, and members of the Citizen's Committee observe in silence as the demolition squad prepares to blast the expensive homes. Some of the owners refuse to evacuate their opulent homes that are doomed to be destroyed by dynamite. Soldiers with bayonets drive the owners out onto the street. In all, three blocks of houses thunderously fall under the ear-shattering explosions. The winds change the direction of the fire northward, toward Fort Mason, where soldiers pump bay water to the fire engines. On the third day of burning hell, the fire dies.

San Francisco is a ruined land of simmering embers and charred bodies. The desolation of the city, where survivors are forced to live and sleep among the unburied dead, is unfathomable to the rest of the world. Slowly, by land and sea, help and provisions arrive. The mayor, with gratitude, notifies Victor that the men and provisions his brother sent have arrived. Victor, Julieta, and Stewart establish a camp for the men and provisions, and they distribute the food to bread lines and the medicine to temporary hospitals.

In her plight to not be driven insane by the crackling sounds of the fire and the cries of those burning alive, Julieta's every waking minute is devoted to helping the survivors. Victor pays a widow handsomely for her late husband's horseless carriage. Cars, which previously were mocked as toys for the rich, are now in demand as the workhorses of the effort. With the car, Victor and Julieta are able to deliver the provisions faster and further away. From the car's window, Julieta hands out bread, fruit, and chocolate to women and children as they drive to drop off provisions to the working men throughout the city who were hired by officials and private owners.

Baby Carriages

The roar of the city's comeback is evidenced by the hundreds of men and soldiers working to clear out the blocks of devastation. The men are grateful to focus on helping the city rebuild while making a living. Because of the shortage of men available to work in the calamity-stricken city, most men earn more rebuilding the city than what they earned at their old jobs before the earthquake. Among the hundreds of honest men working to rebuild the city, there are handfuls of profiteers who charge a premium for their services and for goods that are in short supply but greatly needed. Victor and Julieta stumble upon the owner of a baby carriage store that has not been ruined; he is arguing with a crowd in front of his shop. Baby carriages are in demand for mothers whose arms need a rest, for the comfort of sleeping babies, and as wheels to carry meager belongings. The owner refuses to honor the pre-earthquake price for the carriages, electing instead to sell his merchandise at a premium to the desperate people. This infuriates Victor, and he says to the owner, "You, sir, are morally ruined. Your customers are in dire straits, yet you will not honor your original price. Most merchants, under these horrendous circumstances, would offer a discount as a courtesy."

"On what authority do you meddle in how I run my store?" the merchant complains.

Victor digs into his breast pocket and pulls out a wad of cash. To the amazement of the crowd, one by one, the bills catapult from his hand and land on the counter six feet inside the store. Victor's other hand commands the carriages, one by one, to roll out of the store and stop in front of needy customers.

The merchant's face turns ashen with panic as he realizes that he is dealing with Victor Montenegro, of Montenegro City, a personal acquaintance of the mayor, and he says nothing as he walks into his now empty store and closes the door.

The recipients of the much-needed carriages profusely thank Victor between claps as Julieta studies the warped entryway of the store.

Gold Rush

While a few unscrupulous merchants plot to take advantage of the desperate need of the community, some merchants are honorably making an exceptionally good living and find themselves in the midst of a new gold rush. The earthquake and fires, which many believe are a sign of the end times, encourage many to bury their rancor, do away with petty quarrels, and realign their priorities. For them, facing calamity alone while living under the threat of losing loved ones in the turbulent world is too much to bear. The earthquake and fires separate many through death, but they also bring a historic wave of unification in which countless people unite and reunite. Men race to those jewelers open for business to purchase rings. Couples who had previously opted to wait will not wait for another second and seek out jewelers for their wedding rings. Divorced couples rekindle their love and race to the jewelers. Justices of the peace, pastors, and priests work shifts around the clock to marry and remarry couples who do not want to face another hour of uncertainty without a partner. In the shadow of disaster, love reigns.

The love and peace of the newlyweds are inspiring to those who desperately need a sense of tradition among the rubble of their city. The record number of marriages reminds Victor of his late sister's suggestion that he should propose to Julieta. Victor's late sister's confidence that Julieta would accept his proposal now rings true to Victor. Victor and Julieta are an entertaining powerhouse. As they toured together, he felt her affection for him grow, both on and off the stage. And while Victor is a mystery to Julieta, Victor finds encouragement in Julieta's trust in him. The horrendous earthquake and fires bound them in spirit. And amid so much loss, Victor still has the means to care for Julieta and her family. Julieta—and any other woman, for that matter—would likely accept a marriage proposal from the diplomatic and wealthy illusionist. But Victor cannot bring himself to propose to her, even though his heart demands him to do so. *I will propose when Julieta knows my truth*, he repeats to himself.

The St. Francis caught on fire in the wee hours of the morning. Since then, Juliet has refused to sleep under any roof. Fearing that an aftershock will open up the ground, Julieta is no longer comfortable sleeping on the cot in the mayor's backyard. Victor takes off his dress jacket and tosses it on a branch as a servant hands him a hammock. Victor ties the hammock to two large Victorian box trees as Stewart lies down on Julieta's rejected cot. Victor pulls on the hammock to check that it is secure, and then he says to Julieta, "It is a secure and comfortable hammock."

Julieta sways from exhaustion and steps back. Victor jumps onto the hammock, rocks it, and then assures her, "If it can hold me, it will hold you." Julieta timidly smiles. "Let me help you up," Victor says.

Julieta holds up her arms, and Victor lifts her up onto the hammock. Victor lies back on the hammock. He looks at Julieta, who is sitting next to him, and then he looks up to the sky and says, "A blanket of stars to remind us that there will always be light and not to dwell in darkness. There are as many happy moments to dwell on as there are stars in the universe."

Julieta gazes up to the sky in silence. Exhaustion pulls her down onto the hammock, and she lays her head underneath his outstretched arm. As Victor is about to roll off the hammock, Julieta, drifting into sleep, repositions herself on his open arm and nestles her head against his chest. Victor lays still and stares up at the sky, hoping that the pounding of his heart does not wake her up. His beating heart and the gentle rocking of the hammock do not wake her. He reaches for his dress jacket and drapes it over her, and then he gently wraps his arm around her. He glances at Stewart and sees that he is fast asleep, with his back facing them. Victor feels blessed that during such trying devastation, he has the gift of holding Julieta. Victor is not confused. Due to his monstrosity, he cannot be blessed with mutual love. Julieta can only feel affection, chemistry, and deep care for him. Living in a disaster and seeing the suffering brought on by death at each turn brings people closer. Victor is aware that what Julieta seeks in his arms is a restful sleep, warmth, and security. The wind gently rocks them, but Victor cannot sleep. He wants to keep vigil over Julieta as he treasures holding her close.

In the early morning, earth-crushing explosions awaken them. As the hammock rocks with the explosions, Julieta leans closer to Victor. Victor embraces her as he says, "The officials are dynamiting feeble ruins."

After a light breakfast accompanied by nerve-shattering blasts, Victor and Julieta leave the mayor's house to help hand out provisions and medicine. Stewart is out helping set up tents for a camp in Golden Gate Park for the refugees.

Julieta and Victor spot a woman with tattered clothes and an ashen face walking slowly, tightly holding the hand of a young child. Victor and Julieta walk toward the woman and child to inquire if they have shelter and to suggest where they can go for food. An explosion taking place a block away causes a damaged chimney to teeter toward the path through the street that the woman and child are about to traverse. Victor halts his steps. Julieta stops and follows his concerned gaze. Julieta's warning scream to the woman is drowned out by the sound of another explosion. Victor thrusts his hands up toward the direction of the chimney; with his hands, he commands the chimney to straighten itself and slowly crumble downward. Julieta stares in silence. The chimney that was threatening to brutally bury the woman and her child crumbles down gently, as if the bricks were leaves coasting on the wind.

"Amanda!" yells a man as he leaps over the carcass of a dead horse and piles of rubble to run to embrace the woman and child.

"Papa!" the child shrieks with joy.

As the family walks away, Victor says, "They will be fine."

"You saved their lives."

"Let's continue; there is so much need," Victor says.

Julieta grabs his arm. Victor turns and studies her. Julieta locks her eyes on him and says, "You are rare. I suppose I should not be surprised by your ability to command that chimney. You suspended a large armoire in the air and prevented it from crashing down on me as the ground shook like an angry sea. As I rode the violent earthquake, the armoire remained tranquil above me. You commanded a chimney to gently crumble. How is that possible? In the hallway of that hotel and in this street, there are no smoke and mirrors."

"I will—" Victor begins.

Julieta quickly interrupts, "You confuse me. Carlo Fini also confused me."

"Please, do not tell me you fear me," Victor pleads.

"Fear you? How can I fear you when you saved my life twice?"

"Twice?" Victor asks.

"Yes, twice. When you did not give me up for dead when I fell into a coma, then again in the hotel when the earthquake caught us by surprise," Julieta says with grateful eyes. She continues, "I grew to fear Carlo Fini. In many ways, he was similar to you—charismatic, and an entertainer like you. He possessed a gift for music that he did not share with other talented musicians. You possess a gift that you do not share with other grand illusionists. And believe me when I tell you that in the entertainment world, I have come across many illusionists, but their magic was confined to well-conditioned stages. Julieta studies Victor as explosions echo around them, and then she says, "Your ability is not magic but a power."

"A power," Victor repeats.

"A power that I would not question if it was confined to a stage," Julieta admits.

"Once we depart this apocalyptic nightmare and are back in Montenegro, I will answer all the questions."

"Carlo Fini's legacy is plagued with rumors that he was the devil's instrument, and that is why he was able to compose unworldly music. The intense energy that exudes from you also exuded from him."

The endless smoke twirling up to the sky, blocking the rays of a sun, and the burning scent from the smothering fires cannot cover the overwhelming scent of decay around them. The sounds of the soul-rocking blasts of dynamite are growing closer.

"Let's table this conversation for later and carry on with our rescue mission," Victor suggests.

"I am afraid I would forget this conversation. I am haunted with the feeling that there are episodes that I do not remember. I wake up from dreams horrified, but I cannot recall the details of the dreams. I am tormented with the gnawing feeling that they are not dreams but are memories. I am troubled that I woke up from the coma feeling exhausted, as if I had been running a three-day marathon. I live with a fear that I cannot place."

Julieta gets closer to Victor and anchors her hand on his jacket's lapel, and then she asks, "What am I missing? My heart tells me that you can shed light on my coma and this fear I have."

"I promise you, I will do the impossible to release you from your fear," Victor says.

"Last night as I slept cradled by you on air was the safest I have ever felt. For the first time since waking up from the coma, I was able to sleep a peaceful and fearless sleep. My heart trusts you, but yet my soul is guarded."

A dynamite blast blows a cloud of dust, debris, and burnt embers saturated with the scent of death down on them. Julieta coughs violently to clear the dust and dreadful scent out of her throat as Victor holds on to her arm to steady her. As the dust settles on the rubble around them, Victor pulls out his handkerchief and hands it to the Julieta. Julieta, with a shaking hand, takes the handkerchief from him as she studies Victor's even composure. In her eyes, Victor reads confusion and suspicion.

"Thank you," Julieta says as she wipes away the dust from her eyes. She looks down at the soiled handkerchief and pleads, "I wish to be alone right now."

"As much as I want to respect your wish, this chaotic state is not…"

Julieta walks away from him. Victor watches her walk away as steps hurry up to him.

"Where is Lady Julieta going?" Stewart asks in a worried tone.

"She wishes to be alone," Victor answers as he watches her cross the street.

Their silent watchfulness over Julieta is shattered by the painful yelps of a dog that woke up trapped. Victor and Stewart turn away from the street to the direction of the crying dog caged by rubble. Stewart sees the dog and pulls it free. Their attention to the dog is interrupted by the sound of crashing bricks. Victor crosses the street, in search of Julieta. On the ground, he sees a sliver of the fabric of her dress. The quaking blast of dynamite caused a wall to crash down on Julieta, burying her under a mountain of bricks.

"No!" Victor screams in agony as he races to her on the air, with Stewart following behind. Victor drops to his knees, and his angry hands command the bricks to fly off her. Clutching his handkerchief, Julieta is lying on her side, groaning in pain. Her long chocolate hair is dusted with debris. Blood oozes from the broken skin on her arms, neck, and face. Victor removes his coat, lifts her body up against his, and drapes his coat around her. Victor yells at Stewart to find a coach.

"I am dying, Victor," Julieta utters as she tries to keep her eyes on his.

"No," Victor begs.

Julieta tries to speak again, but instead of words, she coughs up blood.

Victor's body violently shakes as he holds her closer.

"I can save you, but I will not. I do not want to condemn you. God, please do not take her."

Victor feels her hand reach his shoulder and then it slides down his arm. Victor lowers her to look at her face. Her eyes are now closed, and her breath is labored. Victor's gray eyes turn fiery red, and his fangs creep out. Every inch of his body and heart demands that Victor bite her before she draws her last breath. His soul fights against his body and heart. Victor's eyes return to gray, and his fangs recede. Among the ruins in the deserted street, Victor says, "I love you, my Julieta."

Julieta exhales slowly, and then her body loses strength and drapes over his embracing arms. Victor raises her and holds her body close, and as he cradles her, he feels her soul leave her body.

Blood tears rain down from his eyes as the sound of wheels approaches. Stewart exits the car and stands over the inconsolable Victor. In shock, Stewart stares at Julieta's listless body. Stewart grips

Victor's shoulder, and then he pulls back. Victor holds her body close to his to preserve her warmth as his red tears streak down her hair.

"My love for you will never die. Please forgive me for not being there in time to save you from the bricks," Victor tearfully says as he cradles her lifeless body.

Present

The gentle shaking on his arm breaks into Victor's dream. Whiffs of a woman's perfume float through the memory of the scent of decay. He slowly looks up and sees the concerned face of Valentina studying him.

"Mr. Montenegro, pardon me for waking you up, but it appears you were having a bad dream."

Victor straightens up in the Queen Anne chair. Valentina, cradling books on her arm, observes as he presses his hand against his cheek.

"Please have a seat, Miss Santa Cruz," Victor says as he motions to the other Queen Anne chair across from him.

"I was not able to sleep. I came to the library to read, and I must have fallen asleep," Victor explains.

"I came to return these books. I did not realize you were here until I heard you."

"What did you hear?"

"I heard you say, 'Save you from the bricks,'" Valentina says.

Astounded, Victor looks at Valentina in silence.

"I dared to wake you because of the suffering tone in your words."

"Is that all you heard?" Victor asks.

"Those were the only words I could make out. Do you know

what that meant?" Valentina asks.

"Yes, I do. It is a recurring dream."

"There are techniques that can help put an end to recurring dreams," Valentina offers.

"Do you practice those techniques?" Victor asks, studying her.

"No, as an anthropologist, I have an appreciation for dreams. I employ techniques to keep me in a dream state and to try to retain details."

"Do you have nightmares?" Victor asks.

"No. As of late, my dreams have been very lucid and rich with symbolism. When I was a very young child, I would have nightmares of being buried alive. I think those dreams are what inspired me to go into anthropology. When I had those nightmares, my mother would come into my room and sing to me to calm me down," Valentina shares.

"Sing," Victor whispers.

"She sang beautifully; she was the voice of the church choir."

"Do you sing?" Victor asks.

"I can carry a tune, but since my mother's death, I only sing in my dreams."

"You have many talents, Miss Santa Cruz."

"I hope you do not mind me asking, but how long have you been having this nightmare?"

"It is not actually a nightmare; it is a memory of when I lost someone who was very dear to me. From time to time, in my sleep, I relive the moment I lost her."

"Her? How long ago was it that you lost her?" Valentina dares to ask.

"It has been many years."

"I am very sorry," Valentina says.

"Thank you for waking me up, Miss Santa Cruz. Excuse me. I shall see you at dinner. Good day," Victor says as he stands up.

"Good day," Valentina says.

Victor closes the door. Valentina takes the seat he vacated. As she snuggles into the warmth of the chair, she wonders who she was.

Beating Jewel

"Good evening, Miss Santa Cruz," says the butler, Mr. Thompson, as he walks past her carrying Dr. Luque's dress coat and signature hat.

Valentina quickly enters the dining room and finds Dr. Luque sitting in a chair against the wall. Victor is standing with his arm out, and over his open palm is a red heart-shaped jewel the size and color of a medium-size apple. The heart-shaped jewel is beating over Victor's open palm.

As Dr. Luque observes the beating jewel, Victor says, "Doctor."

Dr. Luque protests, "I thought I am here as your guest."

"I believe our souls are the electrical current of our bodies. This heart is strong and capable, with the electrical current from my soul, to pulsate the blood throughout my body. The beauty of this heart is that it is incapable of feeling and unbreakable. I would pay a king's ransom to be able to live with this stone in my chest instead of my heart," Victor says as the heart continues to beat above his hand.

"It is not the right size," Dr. Luque says.

"Good evening," Valentina announces herself.

Dr. Luque notices that the heart over Victor's hand stops beating. The doctor stands up.

"Good evening, Miss Santa Cruz," the doctor welcomes her.

"Nice to see you, Dr. Luque. Joining us for dinner?"

"Yes."

"Your heart is no longer beating," Valentina says.

The heart drops onto Victor's open palm.

"It is a beautiful heart. Is it a jewel?"

"No, it is one hundred percent quartz. Crystal is an excellent conduit for magic," Victor says.

"If it were round, it would be able to foretell the future," Dr. Luque jokes.

"I wish I were enchanted with the future, but I am bewitched by the past—history," Valentina shares.

"Why is that, Miss Santa Cruz? What spell does the past have over you?" Victor asks as he holds out a chair for her at the dining table.

"Thank you," Valentina says as the doctor and Victor join her. "Perhaps it is because humans do not want to be forgotten. This is why we build memorials to the dead. People are survived by their stories. I feel it is my calling to unearth their stories and honor those who precede us."

"Unearth?" Victor asks.

"Yes, for some reason, I am drawn to civilizations that Mother Nature buried alive."

Dr. Luque glances at both of them and encourages, "As someone with the calling to nourish the living, I humbly suggest that we leave the past and future for another time, and enjoy the present company."

"Yes, let's toast to that before the minor arrives to dine with us," Victor says as he motions to the help to serve them their wine.

Ghost Coach

It is after midnight; a cold chill shakes Valentina awake. She sits up to reach for blankets, and she notices the curtains of her balcony doors thrust into her room by an intrusive chill. She gets out of bed and walks to the balcony doors. An image traversing the full moon stops her from closing the doors. She walks out onto the balcony and studies the object that is coming closer as she wraps her arms around her. It is a team of skeleton horses wearing black plumes on their heads and pulling an elegant black coach up to her balcony. The coldness of the night is more frightful to her than the skeleton horses and elegant coached parked on air in front of her. As she investigates the empty coach, a dapperly dressed man jumps off the driver seat, and as he walks on air toward her balcony, he removes his top hat. Valentina is aghast to see that the man is a skeleton. With a wide grin, he bows and then says, "My lady, I am your driver. Mr. Montenegro has sent for you." He puts his top hat back on his skull, and he taps on the balcony railing. The railing parts like French doors, and the skeleton man offers Valentina his hand.

"I am cold," Valentina protests.

He removes his coat and wraps it around Valentina. Valentina can see the outline of his ribs underneath his vest and white shirt.

"I do not want to disappoint Mr. Montenegro," he says.

"It is but a dream," Valentina counsels herself as she grips the skeleton's gloved hand and steps out onto the air and walks into the coach.

From the comfort of the coach, she looks out the window, and her hair trails in the wind as the coach travels toward the moon. As they ride closer to the moon, the brightness is too much for her eyes, and she closes them. When she opens her eyes, the moon's blinding light is gone; instead, she sees ornate tall black gates. The driver opens the coach's door, and he says with a grin, "We have arrived, my lady." Valentina looks out of the coach and up to the moonless sky, and she timidly smiles at the skeleton.

The driver helps Valentina disembark from the coach, and she is relieved to feel the ground, hidden by the crawling fog, underneath her feet. The driver tips his hat, and then he tugs her hand into his arm. With a spring in his step, whistling a song, he escorts Valentina through cathedral gates as they glide open. As Valentina holds firmly to his skeleton arm, her eyes take in the nine magnificent statues of angels with glorious wings. She also notices six trees with weeping foliage standing tall.

"Where are we?" Valentina asks.

Dark clouds float away, uncovering the full moon. The crawling fog recedes, uncovering hundreds of headstones. The full moon's rays light up the marble mausoleums. The craftsmanship of the angels, mausoleums, and headstones harkens back to the ornate graveyards of the turn of the century. The well-nourished lawn, thriving trees, and gates not buried by rust speak of a much-beloved graveyard.

"Mr. Montenegro?" Valentina asks.

"Mr. Montenegro is on his way, my lady."

The grinning driver removes his gloves and tucks them into his trouser pocket. As Valentina studies his skeletal hands, he removes his top hat, and then he balances the brim of the hat on his finger. He blows on his hat, and the hat begins to rapidly spin on his finger.

Valentina is hypnotized by spinning hat, illuminated by the moon.

"In the ocean of eternity," he begins as his hat spins at warping speed, "time will warp for…" He pauses and looks at Valentina and smiles, and then he looks back at his hat, which halts its spinning, and he says, "…love."

Valentina looks at the still hat balanced on his finger, and she repeats, "In the ocean of eternity, time will warp for love."

"Precisely," he says in a delighted tone.

Valentina watches as he walks up the steps of a marble mausoleum trimmed with gold. On the landing, she sees materials for rubbing and a paintbrush but no paint.

He turns and asks, "Would you like to do some rubbing while we wait?"

Valentina turns and looks at the gothic tombstones, rich with symbolism. She turns back to him and says, "Yes."

He picks up the materials and says, "Lead the way, my lady."

Valentina walks past the grandest mausoleum in the graveyard, and she reads the family name etched in gold: *Avila*. Valentina stares at the name for a minute, and then she pulls herself away and walks toward a row of tombstones. She gets on her knees, and he places the materials at her reach. He then takes the paintbrush and sits down a few feet in front of her. Valentina watches as he inserts his hand into the ground and pulls out a skull. He studies the skull, and then he strokes the skull with the paintbrush. Valentina is stunned to see that the brush colors the skull without having been dipped in paint. "I shall spruce up this dearly departed to resemble the sugar skulls I am so fond of because it reminds me of your favorite holiday, All Souls' Day—Day of the Dead."

"How do you know Day of the Dead is my favorite holiday?"

"We are in a graveyard, and you immortalize tombstones of the dead to honor them. It was an educated guess," he says as he continues to paint the skull with different colors.

"Is that a magical paintbrush?"

"Yes. I do not need to carry paint," he answers as he continues to paint.

Valentina begins her rubbing as the skeleton man whistles while decorating the skull.

As Valentina rubs the image of a skull with wings onto the rustling rice paper, the skeleton man's artistic talent comes alive on the aged skull.

"There is beauty in death," the skeleton man says, admiring his painted skull.

Valentina looks up from the tombstone and smiles at him.

"It pleases me greatly that you do not fear me, my lady."

"In studying death, I have become accustomed to seeing skulls," Valentina says.

"Yes, but have you ever met a lively skull?" he asks as he chuckles.

"No. However, this is just a dream."

"Do you really believe this is a dream?" he asks as he puts down his painted skull and pulls another skull from the ground.

Valentina looks up at him, and then she looks at the painted skull resting on the moist grass. She notices that not one inch of the skull is bare. She studies the skeleton man as he begins to decorate the second skull.

He looks up from the skull and says to her, "Bodies may be in separate coffins, but loving souls are never separated."

Valentina continues her rubbing, and then she asks, "What is your name?"

Not getting a response, she looks up to see him standing next to Victor.

"His name is Stewart Van Green," Victor says as he offers his hand.

Valentina anchors on his hand to stand up.

"Thank you, Stewart," Victor says as he removes Stewart's jacket from Valentina and hands it back to him.

Stewart removes his top hat and bows at Valentina.

Victor removes his dress jacket and places it on her. He offers her his arm. Valentina holds onto his arm, and he escorts her to an ornate bench.

"There is something I need to ask you, Miss Santa Cruz," Victor says.

Valentina wraps his coat tighter around her, and she turns to face him.

"Yes, Mr. Montenegro?"

"It is my understanding that you have not dedicated your study to one particular branch of anthropology."

"That is correct. I am fascinated with all branches of anthropology."

"It is my hope that you realize your goals. Teo is very fond of you, and he is excelling under your tutelage. It is my hope that you stay on as long as you can as his teacher."

"Thank you, Mr. Montenegro. Teo is a wonderful student, and I care about him deeply."

Victor smiles tenderly at Valentina.

"Is that what you want to ask me? About anthropology?"

"What is your anthropological opinion on the belief in mythical creatures?"

"Do you want to know the prevailing opinion or my conclusion?" Valentina asks.

"I would like to know your opinion, Miss Santa Cruz," Victor says, studying her.

Valentina admires his gray eyes, which tenderly study her, and without breaking eye contact, she admits, "It is very compelling that distinct cultures cut off from one another by language, geographical distance, and time period share the same beliefs in certain creatures. A good example is ghosts. I have yet to come across a culture or time period in history where the idea of ghosts does not exist. Belief in ghosts is prevalent due to the innumerable witness accounts. Therefore, my conclusion, based on the countless reports worldwide and throughout time, is that ghosts do exist."

Victor smiles tenderly at her and says, "I agree with your conclusion. I feel your philosophy would also support the notion that demons exist as well."

"I will not argue against it, which is disconcerting, as demons are the most fearsome of mythical creatures."

"More fearsome than vampires?"

"Yes," Valentina replies.

Victor lifts her hand up to his lips and lovingly kisses it. Valentina's overwhelmed, loudly beating heart startles her awake. She sits up in her bed and looks at her closed balcony doors and sees the light of day. Sadness washes over her as she tells herself it was just a dream.

Teo's enthusiasm for her lesson on the classification of animals lifts her spirits. Valentina feels blessed to be teaching a child who is hungry for knowledge, and his attention keeps her mind off the dream. Movement out in the hallway makes her look up at the clock, and she realizes that it is time to end the lessons for today.

She follows Teo and his nanny to the bustling kitchen, where Teo enjoys doing his homework while he has a snack. Miss Ruiz, who is at the fire pit, attending to a roasting pig, says, "Good afternoon." They wish her a good afternoon, and Miss Ruiz looks at Teo and says, "My son, your snack is on the table."

Weeks have passed since Valentina's arrival to Montenegro. She has become accustomed to the grandness of the estate, she appreciates the warm formality of the staff, and she is in sync with the schedule of the house. But what she is still getting used to is seeing the pit roasting of whole pigs and whole turkeys, the firing up of enormous cauldrons of soups and stewing pots of sauces, and the warming up of decadent desserts. With such a huge staff and constant visitors, a stove will not do to feed so many.

Valentina helps herself to some watermelon agua fresca. She then removes the scrunchie from her wrist and ties her long black hair into a ponytail. She walks up to the pit and looks at the succulent pig and inhales the delicious smell. "It smells divine, Miss Ruiz," she says.

Valentina turns sideways to face Miss Ruiz, who is hanging a pot to boil potatoes. To the surprise of everyone in the kitchen, they hear Victor and Dr. Luque enter the kitchen through the back door. Valentina turns her head to greet Victor and the doctor, who join them at the pit. Dripping grease from the roasting pig causes the fire in the pit to flare up, and it catches the tip of her ponytail. Victor immediately wraps his hand on her burning hair and smothers the flame. The sound of the crackling fire echoes in the kitchen as everyone stares at Victor as he drapes her ponytail over her shoulder, away from the fire. He takes hold of her elbow and pulls the shaken Valentina away from the pit.

"That is why I am not allowed near fire," Teo says, breaking the silence.

"Permit me," Dr. Luque says as he examines her back with his hand.

"Your shirt doesn't appear to be burned. Do you feel your back burning?" Dr. Luque asks Valentina.

Without removing her eyes from Victor, she responds, "No, Doctor. Thank you."

"Are you fine?" Victor asks.

"Yes. How is your hand?" Valentina asks as she looks to the doctor for reassurance.

"No need to worry about his hand. This is not the first time he has wrangled fire," Dr. Luque assures her.

"Thank goodness the fire did not engulf your whole head," Miss Ruiz says.

"Yes," Valentina agrees with a smile.

She looks at the charred tip of her ponytail. The smell of her burned hair rattles her. She looks up to Victor's concerned eyes.

"I was due for a trim," Valentina says with a trembling smile.

"It will grow back," Miss Ruiz says.

Mrs. Walker enters the kitchen, and Victor offers, "Mrs. Walker is a licensed hairstylist. She can trim your hair."

"Thank you," Valentina says as she follows Mrs. Walker.

Mrs. Walker leads her into the drawing room and motions for her to sit on the stool. She pulls her scissors and combs out of a desk drawer.

"You no longer see clients?" Valentina asks.

"I fell and injured my shoulder, and that prevents me from cutting hair for a living. As Mr. Montenegro's head housekeeper, I oversee the housekeeping staff, which does not require much use of my shoulder. While I value my employment here, I do miss cutting hair. However, when my shoulder is not giving me a hard time, I cut the hair of the staff members," Mrs. Walker says as she lowers Valentina's scrunchie to a couple of inches above the burned tip and cuts it off, placing it on a table near her.

As she combs out Valentina's hair, she says, "I am sorry you had to experience that, but I am glad it was not worse. Your hair will grow back."

"If it were not for Mr. Montenegro..." Valentina expresses.

"You would be dripping agua fresca, which was the closest cool liquid," Mrs. Walker says.

"I hope you do not mind me asking, but how did you come to be employed by Mr. Montenegro?"

"Like everyone in this house, including you, through

recommendation. My husband is an accountant, and he worked for Dr. Luque Senior, and now he works for his son, Dr. Mario Luque."

"Mr. Montenegro is a very private man," Valentina sighs.

"Yes, very private."

Mrs. Walker cut off three inches. Her hair still cascades down her back, but it is lighter and has a bounce to it when she moves her head. Valentina does not like her new length, and she will eagerly wait for it to grow back.

"Thank you, Mrs. Walker," Victor says as she places Valentina's hair on the palm of the hand that smothered the fire.

Mrs. Walker leaves his bedroom. Victor stares at the hair, still gathered by her scrunchie. The crisp ends of the strands of her hair upset Victor more than he expected. The safety and well-being of all in his household are of great concern to him, but Valentina being inches away from getting seriously hurt causes a strong desire to protect her to grow within him. He is not sure what compelled him to ask Mrs. Walker to give him her hair. But as it rests on his hand, he is reminded that hair not exposed to the elements can remain in its present state for a hundred years—a part of her he can hold on to once she is gone. He places her hair in a wooden box for safekeeping.

Dinner will not be ready for another thirty minutes. Valentina decides to visit the mansion's octagon-shaped library to borrow a book to read after dinner. As she reaches the library's open door, she hears Victor speaking in the library.

"Explain to me, Doctor...I believe a person can die from a broken heart, but science will argue that it is not possible to die from a broken heart because love is an affair of the brain, not the heart."

Dr. Luque walks to stand by the unlit fireplace, which is framed by two massive winged lions, and he says, "Well, that theory is supported by those suffering from memory loss who do not remember or recognize their loved ones, and MRI scans indicate that love lights up the pleasure center of the brain."

"In recent years, the theory of broken heart syndrome is once again raising the debate that a person can die from a broken heart," Valentina says as she enters the library.

Victor and Dr. Luque turn to greet her.

"Please forgive me for entering into your conversation; the door was open."

"Welcome," Victor says as he warmly looks at her.

"Quite right, broken heart syndrome," Dr. Luque says.

Valentina looks into Victor's eyes, which hold her gaze, and she says, "I hope you are not suffering from a heart ailment, Mr. Montenegro."

Victor is moved by the concerned tone in her voice, "I assure you, Miss Santa Cruz, aside from light-induced migraines, I am of robust health."

"I am very pleased to hear that," Valentina says in a low tone, wishing she was more convinced.

"Victor, as an illusionist, has a keen interest in wrangling with science. Manipulating the elements adds magic," Dr. Luque assures her.

Valentina looks at the unlit fireplace.

"This is the first time I have seen the fireplace unlit. I hope it is not on account of me. I assure you that I am fine. In fact, I love this fireplace," Valentina says.

Victor, snapping his fingers, produces a match. He then strikes the match in midair and throws the lit match into the fireplace; the fireplace instantly contains a roaring fire.

Dr. Luque studies how Victor admires Valentina as she smiles in awe at how quickly Victor lit the fire.

"Amazing, thank you," Valentina says.

Victor smiles, "My pleasure, Miss Santa Cruz."

"I came to borrow a book. I will not take long," Valentina says.

"I am suddenly depressed to think that people could die of a broken heart. I think I am going to pour myself some brandy. Miss Santa Cruz, Victor, care to join me?" Dr. Luque offers as he walks to the Gothic Revival carved oak bar.

"Miss Santa Cruz, will you join us for a predinner brandy?" Victor invites.

Valentina smiles, "It would be a pleasure."

Dr. Luque pours the brandy and hands them their glasses. He picks up his glass, raises it, and says, "Let's drink to health and whole hearts."

Victor clinks his glass against Valentina's and says, "To good health."

They sip their drinks.

"Let's get comfortable," Victor says as he motions toward the two leather sofas and leather Queen Anne. Valentina sits down on the Queen Anne, and Victor and Dr. Luque sit across from each other on separate sofas.

"Doctor, do you have knowledge of cardiology?" Valentina asks.

"Not particularly. I mostly practice general medicine. I have experience in osteology."

"Right. When we met when I first arrived, Mr. Montenegro said you know your way around bones," Valentina says, leaning forward.

"My late uncle was a forensic osteologist, and I would assist him. I learned a great deal from him."

"Fascinating. I am leaning more toward forensic and cultural anthropology."

"So you are planning to return to school?" Dr. Luque asks.

"I have a degree in mathematics, which served me well to find a job in finance, but my love for anthropology never waned. I decided to work as a private tutor so that I have weeks off in the year to pursue my anthropology interests. Before returning to school, I need to first decide on a branch of anthropology."

"I must admit that I did find it exciting to assist my late uncle as he solved crimes involving deaths. However, my calling is to help prolong life. My door as a physician and an amateur anthropologist will always be open."

"Thank you, Doctor," Valentina says with a big smile.

"Dr. Luque is being modest. His knowledge is vast, and he is a specialist doctor. He mostly practices general medicine because he is the Montenegros' private doctor, just like his father was. The good doctor is on call for everyone living in my estate or working for me. I wish you well, but if you are in need of a doctor, Dr. Luque is very capable."

"Thank you, Mr. Montenegro and Dr. Luque," Valentina says.

"It is the romance of making house calls that keeps me under Montenegro's employment," Dr. Luque jokes.

They hear bells chiming throughout the house.

"Dinner will soon be served," Victor says.

"Another perk of being Montenegro's private doctor—Miss Ruiz's succulent cooking," Dr. Luque says.

Coffins

Valentina looks out her living room window up to the afternoon sky. Thick gray clouds are rolling toward the mansion. Valentina is frustrated that since she has arrived, rarely has she seen blue skies. She is looking forward to the passing of the unusual weather, but for now, she will chance rain for a bit of fresh air in the mansion's sprawling garden, which features an enchanting maze. She grabs her cell phone and a forensic anthropology book. In the hallway on her way to the back of the mansion, her cell phone rings. As Valentina answers the phone, Victor and Dr. Luque, engaged in conversation, walk toward Valentina. Their conversation is halted by Valentina's excited tone.

"Yes! It will be my pleasure to assist. This is incredible. I understand, I will get there as fast I can. Thank you for calling me."

Valentina looks up to see Victor and Dr. Luque approaching.

"Mr. Montenegro, can I ask Mr. Simms for a ride?"

"I am sorry, but Jules is driving Mrs. Walker home. He will not be back for another thirty minutes."

Valentina frowns in thought.

"I'm pressed for time. I shall call a taxi."

"Is there a problem?" Victor asks, concerned.

"Coffins were unearthed at the Richardson estate. The anthropologists need urgent assistance to categorize and record the discovery. They are pressed for time due to the storm coming in, and they must secure the site because they do not know if it is a crime scene or an abandoned burial ground."

"The Richardson estate? Interesting. Why is there a shortage of help?" Dr. Luque asks.

"Most of the local anthropologists flew to Indonesia to study the lost kingdom that was recently discovered, hidden under layers of volcano ash," Victor says.

"Yes," Valentina says, surprised that Victor is aware of the lost kingdom.

"I will be happy to drive you there, Miss Santa Cruz," Victor says.

"Great! Thank you," Valentina says.

"I would like to volunteer to help in any capacity that I can," Dr. Luque offers.

"That would be great," Valentina says, welcoming Dr. Luque.

Valentina is excited that she will be at the site of a curious discovery, studying it alongside seasoned anthropologists. But her excitement does not overshadow her thrill of sitting in the passenger seat of Victor's personal car. It is the Phantom that normally transports her, but today, she has the privilege to ride in Victor's Bentley with him in the driver's seat.

"This is a very nice car, Mr. Montenegro," Valentina says with a shy smile.

"This is his errand car—for when he needs to drive to the store for milk," Dr. Luque teases.

"The other cars only fit two people, and Mario does not like riding in the trunk," Victor says.

Valentina's laughter at his remark makes Victor smile with delight.

Dr. Luque notices Victor's beaming smile.

"How did you know about the lost kingdom?" Valentina asks.

"I heard about it during a meeting of international diplomats," Victor answers.

"Do you wish you had discovered it?" Dr. Luque asks.

Valentina looks back at Dr. Luque, puzzled by his question.

"Victor is not just an ardent treasure hunter; he also seeks lost cities," Dr. Luque says.

"There are other lost cities waiting to be discovered," Victor says to Dr. Luque, and then he looks at Valentina with a smile and says, "Would you like to be part of one of my expeditions?"

"I would love to, yes!" Valentina beams.

Victor smiles triumphantly at her response, which does not escape Dr. Luque's attention.

They arrive at the Richardson estate, which is covered by a dark gray sky, with billowing clouds and balmy winds. They see a couple of patrol cars and four officers guarding the site. Archaeologists are busy excavating as anthropologists survey and take notes.

Gina, the anthropologist who called Valentina, walks to the trio to greet them.

"Thank you for coming, Valentina," Gina says.

"Gina, this Mr. Montenegro and Dr. Luque. Dr. Luque is a doctor with knowledge of forensic anthropology, and he has offered to help."

"Excellent. While we wait for the archeologists to finish excavating, you and I can start with examining the grounds for any historical clues or evidence of a crime."

"Valentina, do you know how to use the GPR—the ground-penetrating radar?" Gina asks.

"Yes, I do," Valentina confirms.

Gina points to an eight-foot stone wall near the burial area. "This is a wall of great interest. A local historian shared the local suspicion that there is a hidden passage near the wall. I will take this end of the wall, and you take the other. Run the GPR alongside the wall, and also study the wall itself for any markings or abnormalities."

Gina smiles at Dr. Luque and says, "Let me introduce you to the archaeologists; they could use your assistance with the bodies."

Valentina gets the GPR ready.

"I am going to acknowledge the officers. Then I will leave you to work. Please call me if you need a ride back," Victor says to Valentina.

"Thank you, Mr. Montenegro," Valentina says with a smile.

Valentina does not get too far with the GPR when she looks up and notices that one of the huge stones on the wall has two small stones protruding from it. She turns off the GPR, and as Victor is about to drive away, she pushes the two small stones. The ground below her pulls away, and she drops four feet. Victor jumps out of his car and races to her. Her shock at dropping down so suddenly is replaced by the excitement of discovering that she landed on top of a wooden hatch.

"Valentina, are you all right?" Victor asks, concerned.

"I think I found the hidden pathway," Valentina says, knocking on the hatch with her fist.

"That is great, but are you sure you are not hurt?"

"Yes, I am fine."

Victor straightens up.

Valentina stands up. As her eyes scan the hatch under her feet, thrilled by the discovery, she asks, "Do you see Gina close by?"

Victor walks away from the opening that swallowed Valentina to search for Gina. He then hears the sound of stones cracking. Valentina yells out in horror. Victor looks up in time to see the section of the wall over Valentina about to tumble down on her. Victor immediately runs to the wall and rams his side against the crumbling stones. The wall tilts away from her direction, falling to the other side. It takes a moment for Valentina to realize that Victor stopped the wall from crashing down on her. She knows that she saw the wall starting to lean over her, with its top layer of stones beginning to break away. She is amazed and mystified that Victor was able to change the direction of the fall of the stone wall, weighing a ton, and stop the stones from burying her alive.

Dr. Luque, Gina, and the officers race to them, stunned by what has just occurred.

Victor pulls up Valentina. Valentina, terrorized by how close she was to death, tightly embraces Victor with great gratitude. Victor, shaken that Valentina was close to being buried under a heap of old stones, holds her close. As he holds the trembling Valentina, Victor is struck by a feeling of overwhelming familiarity, as if he has held her close before. The two embrace in silence as Gina, Dr. Luque, and the officers investigate the crumbled wall and the passage in the ground. After a minute, Dr. Luque puts his attention on Victor and Valentina. He can see Valentina trembling in his arms, and he notices that while Victor's arms comfort her, there is confusion in his concerned expression, as if he is lost.

Victor, without letting her go, gently pulls away from her embrace, and as he studies her face, he asks, "Are you all right?"

Still shaken, she struggles to answer. She locks eyes with Victor as if she is afraid he will disappear.

"Permit me," Dr. Luque says.

Victor slowly lets her go.

Dr. Luque checks her pupils, and as he begins to examine her head for signs of trauma, Valentina says, "I am fine, Doctor."

She looks at Victor and gratefully reports, "Not one stone touched me. Thank you, Mr. Montenegro."

"There is still a lot of work to do. Thank you again, Mr. Montenegro," Valentina says, turning back to the wall.

"Leave the wall and underground passage for now. The city's engineers are on their way to stabilize the rest of the wall and check the safety of the passage," an officer says.

Valentina gives Victor a smile, and she follows Gina to the group of archaeologists, who returned to their post when they saw that no one was hurt.

"I will keep an eye on her and make sure she gets home," Dr. Luque says to Victor as he watches Valentina walk toward the archaeologists.

"I know you are a strong man, but it was not just your weight that stopped that wall from—"

"Burying her," Victor says.

"Your weight and power saved her, and thank God for that. But what puzzles me is that you hid your power behind your strength. Why?"

"I do not want to scare her," Victor says. He shakes Dr. Luque's hand, and he implores, "Keep her safe," as he turns to leave.

Victor sends the chauffeur, Jules Simms, to the site to wait for Valentina.

It is close to dinner when Valentina returns to the mansion. She is greeted by Mrs. Walker, who informs her, "Mr. Montenegro will not be home for dinner."

Teo, holding a deck of cards, comes running up to Valentina and says, "Uncle Monty needs to work on a treat."

"A treat?" Valentina asks.

"A treaty," Mrs. Walker corrects.

"Were you gardening?" Teo asks.

"No, I was doing some anthropology work. I am sorry to miss dinner, but as you can see, I am very dusty and need to take a shower. Please have dinner with your nanny and the staff," Valentina apologizes.

The shower washes away the dirt, but it does not calm her nerves.

She ponders the events of the exciting day—the spiritual high that comes from assisting archaeologists and anthropologists; the invigorating sense of accomplishment for locating the rumored underground passage; the terrifying jolt of the crumbling wall; Victor's breathtaking strength that saved her from being buried under the stones. She relives the intoxicating memory of Victor holding her close as she drifts to sleep.

As soon as she falls asleep, she dreams of seeing herself buried under a pile of bricks. She is pulled out from under the bricks, and she looks down at her body and notices that she is wearing a Victorian dress. She cannot see the man who is holding her, but feeling his heart breaking from grief over her startles her awake. She sits up and grabs her journal and writes down her dream. Since she was a child, she has dreamed of being buried alive. She does not know why she would dream that as a child, but now, as a budding anthropologist, she wants to believe that her dreams of being buried alive stem from her work in the field. This dream is interesting to her because of the Victorian dress. She makes a note to check with the archaeologists to see if the remains at the Richardson estate date back to the turn of the century. She puts down her journal. As she falls back to sleep, she prays that Victor treasures their embrace as much as she is treasuring it.

"Good morning, Doctor."

Dr. Luque quickly closes the curtains on his huge double windows.

"Good morning, Doctor." Dr. Luque says.

"I have a gift for you, my esteemed colleague," Suzette says.

Dr. Luque smiles as she hands him a small jar of blood.

"Werewolf blood?" Dr. Luque hopes.

"Yes, this time, I brought you domestic werewolf blood, so you can compare it to the foreign werewolf blood."

"Thank you so much. Please have a seat. Would you care for coffee, tea, or water?"

"No, thank you," Suzette says as she sits down on the comfortable oversized leather couch.

Dr. Luque walks to the refrigerator, places the werewolf blood in the back, and pulls out a small jar.

"This is a token of my appreciation," Dr. Luque says as he hands her the jar.

"That is very kind of you, a jar of human blood for my refreshment."

"Do not ask where I got it from," Dr. Luque says with a laugh.

"I hope you are seeing to it that Victor is getting the blood he needs, not just rodent blood. He was not at Wolf Tower last night," Suzette says, concerned.

"Yesterday was an exciting day for him. We accompanied Miss Santa Cruz to an archaeology site. Victor stopped a wall from crushing down on her, essentially saving her life."

"He saved her from falling stones?" Suzette asks as she gets off the couch and stands face to face with Dr. Luque.

"Yes, and then later that night, he had to deal with a treaty."

Dr. Luque looks into Suzette's eyes and then asks, "Are you feeling like yourself?"

"Yes. The trip to Wolf Tower for werewolf blood did me wonders. Why?"

"No evolutions?"

"What do you mean, Doctor?" Suzette asks, puzzled.

"How is your heart?"

"My heart is doing its job—pumping blood throughout my system for rejuvenation and vigor."

"Hmmm," Dr. Luque thinks.

"Doctor, stop treating me as a patient; consult with me."

"Victor has been talking a lot about the heart," Dr. Luque shares.

"We all do, Doctor. We often lament to one another about our inability to have mutual love. A vampire's heart has the energy to continue to thrive for time eternal, but it does not have the light of love. We have conquered mortality; now we seek true love—mutual love," Suzette says.

"Right," Dr. Luque nods sympathetically.

Suzette studies him for a while, and then she says with regret, "Victor has not allowed me to put him under the Amare trance. The Amare trance will make you feel as if you are in love with the person who is in love with you, if only for a short, precious time. The Amare trance is our escape. It is what makes us feel human."

Dr. Luque looks down.

"Victor speaking about the heart gives me hope. If ever we can find our way back to mutual love, I pray he falls in love with me. He knows I am in love with him. We have a history, and we have been intimate," Suzette says.

"Have you been intimate with him recently, Suzette?"

Suzette sits on the examination table.

"No," Suzette whispers.

"According to science, you do not exist. Therefore, science cannot find a pathway to mutual love. As it is now, the debate as to whether love is an affair of the heart or the brain continues," Dr. Luque says.

"Yes, I've read the research on broken heart syndrome."

"I think it is a strong argument. People throughout the ages have spoken of the heart being broken over love," Dr. Luque says.

"For a vampire to meet his or her demise as a result of a broken heart would be a poetic end. There is nothing poetic about brutal destruction."

Blood tears trail down her cheeks. Dr. Luque quickly grabs a

Victorian tear vial and catches her tears.

"Doctor, you have horrendous bedside manner," Suzette says, trying to be humorous as her tears continue to travel into the vial.

"Your tears of sadness could quite possibly hold the key to your quest for mutual love."

Dr. Luque tightly closes the vial and puts it in the refrigerator. He walks back to Suzette and wraps his arms around her, and she clings to him as she cries her blood tears for Victor's inability to love her into his crisp white lab coat.

Valentina is saddened by the news that Victor will not dine in the mansion. She was hoping they would have dinner so that she could share the developments at the Richardson estate. She expects that Victor will not disclose how he managed to stave off a ton of stones. She will have to settle for the privilege of being enchanted by his strength, which is as enthralling as his magical prowess. When Victor prevented a wall weighing a ton from crashing down on her and killing her, it was powerful and spectacular, but it also awoke in her a feeling that confuses her. When she thinks about the incident, a sense of dread crashes down on her. She tells herself that she is still reeling from almost dying at the site. The wall is no longer a threat, yet still, as she thinks about her dreams of being buried alive, she worries that it might be a warning.

Suzette embraces Victor tightly in the privacy of his bedroom. Victor warmly holds her, and then he asks, "Is there something wrong?"

Suzette, without releasing her embrace, says, "I miss you dearly."

Victor wraps his arms tighter around her as Suzette breathes out, "Thank you, my love."

After a minute, he releases her. He looks at her and says, "You look beautiful."

"Thank you, but when I first arrived, you told me that I look beautiful. Did you forget that you already complimented me? Perhaps I should be asking you whether something is wrong."

"You do look beautiful," Victor says with a smile.

Suzette walks to the loveseat and reaches into the gift bag that she had placed there when they first entered into the privacy of his bedroom. From the gift bag, she pulls out a big jar of werewolf blood.

"You did not visit Wolf Tower last night. I did not want you to wait until the next full moon for werewolf blood. It is domestic," she says, handing the jar to him.

Victor takes the bottle with one hand, and with his other hand he clasps Suzette's hand and showers it with kisses as he says, "Thank you for thinking about me."

"I always think about you, my love," Suzette says, wishing he would shower her lips with kisses.

Victor walks to his desk, places the jar in a big drawer, and locks it.

"You are not going to drink it?"

"If I drink it now, I will not be able to eat."

"Right," she confirms.

"We have a few minutes. Please, have a seat," Victor says as he leads her to one of the loveseats next to a round table facing the fireplace.

Victor walks to the unlit fireplace, leans against the huge side column, and puts his hands into his pockets.

"How is Ivan?" Victor asks.

"He is fine," Suzette answers.

"I am going to call him; I have a lead on a treasure."

"I am sure he will be happy to hunt with you," Suzette says.

"He is a good man," Victor expresses.

"Yes, he is a wonderful man. But I am here with Victor Montenegro. Let's talk about us," Suzette pleads.

"Suzette, I..."

"Is there someone new in your life? You know I will understand. Just tell me," Suzette says.

Victor walks to the bookshelf on the other side of the room, pulls out a book, and puts it on his desk. He then answers, "I have not met anyone recently."

Suzette reaches into her purse and pulls out the fan he gave to her over a century ago and gently fans herself.

"Do you need a new fan?" Victor asks her, walking back to the fireplace column.

"I had the witch who was commissioned by Ivan to enchant my mirror so that I can see my reflection also enchant the fan so that it will maintain its luster and usage," Suzette says, pressing the fan against her heart.

"It gives me peace to know that Ivan will always be there for you," Victor says.

"This is emotionally exhausting," Suzette says, staring down at her fan.

"We are all emotionally tired. Henrietta, Ivan, you and I, and every other vampire are perpetually exhausted. Any vampire who disagrees either has a stone for a heart or is a denying fool. We live longer than a body should. Our longevity exposes us to much suffering in the world. Our souls are deprived of the light. The fleeting moments of happiness are few and far between compared to the constant sorrow and horror of being a monster," Victor says.

Suzette gets up and walks to him. She rests both of her hands on his chest and leans into him. "As a woman of science, as a creature born by God's grace, as the woman who deeply loves you, there is not a day that goes by that I don't try to find a way to set your soul free," Suzette says.

"Science is only equipped to handle nature. Our existence is against nature. We are no longer creatures of God but the devil's monsters. My sister passed with a prayer on her lips for my salvation. I continue to roam through time, fearing that God has forsaken me. I hope my sister rests in peace and that she is not tortured by my torment. The day I buried Julieta, I also buried my only chance for happiness. It seems that while half of our hearts are capable of love, our vampire blood damns any chance of love."

"Does my love for you no longer mean anything to you?" Suzette asks, pulling away from him to look up at his eyes.

"I respect your love for me, and I care for you deeply."

Victor looks at the clock on his nightstand, "Let's start our evening."

"We have time to discuss the dark side of being vampires, but a fairytale night awaits us," Suzette says with an encouraging smile.

Victor smiles and nods as he walks to open the door. They leave his bedroom, and when they reach the top of the stairs, they pause to watch as Teo is about to perform a card trick, to the delight of Valentina, at the bottom of the stairs. Teo, minding his presentation, hands a card to Valentina for her to inspect. Valentina, satisfied that the card has not been tampered with, returns the card to the excited Teo.

With much showmanship, and much to his own amazement, Teo succeeds in making the card spin underneath his hand. Valentina's big smile cheers him on. He then makes the card spin between his hands, then he puts the spinning card under one hand, and then he snaps his fingers, and the card disappears. Teo, squealing with accomplishment, bows.

Valentina wholeheartedly applauds.

Victor proudly applauds. Teo looks up the stairs, and with excitement, he asks, "Did you see me do the trick, Uncle Monty?"

"Yes, I did. Well done, son. I am very proud of you."

Valentina's heart stops when she sees he is not alone. She turns and gives the proud Teo a hug as Victor and Suzette descend the stairs.

"How did you do that, Teo?" Valentina asks.

"A magician never tells," Teo proudly asserts.

"That is right, son. A magician never tells," Victor says as he smiles at Valentina.

"Since the day you were born, I knew you were magical," Suzette says as she caresses Teo's hair.

Teo smiles at her and respectfully pulls away as he says, "Thank you, Dr. Suzette."

"Good evening. Nice to see you again, Doctor," Valentina says.

"How are you, Miss Santa Cruz?"

"I am fine, thank you. I hope you two will enjoy your evening," Valentina says as she takes hold of Teo's hand.

"Yes. We are going to the opera," Suzette says, and then she takes Victor's arm and declares, "It will be a fairytale evening."

"Lovely," Valentina says.

"It is our sponsor night," Victor clarifies.

As Valentina puts her attention on him, she fights to keep a professional demeanor. She does not want him to know that the idea of Victor going out with Suzette is making her feel ill.

"Sponsor night?" Valentina asks.

"In the late sixteenth century, our ancestors began to sponsor orphaned young ladies to have a night at the opera, which was intended to introduce them to cultural arts and to young men of well standing for marriage. In this century, we continue the custom. We invite young ladies to the opera and purchase their elegant gowns, just as our ancestors did, but instead of introducing them to young men of well standing, we give them four-year scholarships to the university of their choosing," Suzette says proudly.

"You are related," Valentina says with a smile.

"Not blood relatives," Victor admits.

"His family and my family have a beautiful history spanning centuries," Suzette says as she tenderly looks at Victor.

"We do not want to keep the young ladies waiting to start their enchanted evening," Victor says to Suzette.

"It is a great service you are doing for those young ladies," Suzette says.

Victor pulls away from Suzette and walks over to Teo, picks him up, and gives him a hug. He then puts him down and says, "I am very proud of you, son. Keep up your grades, and I will teach you another trick. Have a good night, son."

Teo hugs Victor's middle and says, "Thank you, Uncle Monty."

"Teo Montenegro," his nanny calls out to him.

"Go to Miss Peterson, son."

Valentina watches Victor as he watches Teo dash to his nanny.

Victor then turns to meet her gaze, and he tenderly smiles as he tips his top hat to her and says, "I wish you a good evening."

"Good evening," Valentina says to Victor with a smile.

Suzette walks over to Victor and hooks her arm into his.

Valentina looks at Suzette tightening her grip on Victor's now bent arm, and then Valentina says, "Good night, Doctor."

"Have a nice evening, Miss Santa Cruz."

Suzette's flowing dress caressing Victor's tuxedo leg bothers Valentina. She feels threatened by their historical family bond.

Victor patiently looks on as Suzette twirls around the hotel suite. After the third twirl, she stops. She looks at Victor, who is leaning on his walking stick, and says with delight, "The opera was divine! The joyful look in the eyes of the four young ladies was heartwarming. Having you at my side all evening was a dream."

"It was a pleasure. We are fortunate to be able to help the young ladies secure an education that will serve them well."

"Yes, and they will never forget this evening—their princess night. Us being here in this century is a blessing for them," Suzette says as she studies him.

"I have done my gentlemanly duty to see you safely to your suite, my lady," Victor says as he tips his hat.

"Please do not go," Suzette pleads.

"It has been an exciting night; you should rest," Victor says.

"Have a drink with me, and let us watch the morning sun's red, purple, and orange rays break through the dark sky."

"Too much alcohol will thin out your blood," Victor says, excusing himself.

"I will not die from diluted blood. What is killing me is my heart because you do not acknowledge my love for you. I respected your love for Julieta, may she rest in peace. I respected your need to mourn her loss. You here in Montenegro and me in New Orleans has afforded you plenty of space from me. I am not asking for a relationship. I only wish to love you."

"Suzette, please understand…"

"You understand how painful unrequited love is. It not only crushes the heart, but it tortures the soul," Suzette says.

"We are condemned. I cannot love you. Our monster hearts are not suited for love, just pain."

"How about your needs as a man, Victor?" Suzette asks.

Victor turns away, rests his walking stick against a chair, and walks to the bar.

"What would you like to drink?" Victor offers.

"Is there someone in your life?"

"I have not met anyone new," Victor says as he pours himself some brandy.

"But is there someone in your life now?"

Victor stares into his drink.

"Victor," Suzette begs.

"I do not know how to answer that," Victor admits.

Suzette inhales through the pain in her chest. She caresses her earring, which Victor had salvaged from a sunken treasure and given to her years ago. Victor takes a sip of his drink as he watches as she removes the pin from her hair. Her hair cascades down onto her bare shoulders.

"Do you still think I am beautiful?" Suzette asks.

"As beautiful as the first day I met you," Victor says, and he takes another sip of his drink.

"I have a wish," Suzette sweetly says.

"A wish?"

Suzette scans her enormous suite, and she looks over to Victor and says, "I do not like this distance. Next time I will not get a suite; I need something more intimate."

She curls up her leg up to remove her shoe, and she loses her balance. Victor, using magic, catches her before she hits the floor. As she straightens back up from his magical hold, Suzette says, "You know that a fall will not kill me, yet your instinct was to save me. You care that I do not fall."

"It would hurt you. I do not want to see you hurt," Victor says.

"I love you, Victor."

"Get some rest," Victor says in a kind voice as he puts down his drink.

Suzette's heart races at the thought of him leaving.

"My wish is that you carry me to bed," Suzette supplicates.

Victor lifts her off her feet.

"Stop! Put me down."

Victor lowers her back to her feet.

Suzette rests a hand on her chest and pleads, "Not with magic. Carry me to bed like a man."

Victor pulls his hat lower over his eyes and looks down as he stands at the bar. Suzette presses her hand against her pounding heart. After a few painful seconds, she kicks off her other shoe to break the silence. Victor looks up, and their eyes meet. He removes his hat and places it on the bar. She watches his every step toward her. Once in front of her, he stops to look into her sad eyes, and then he lifts her into his arms. Suzette's heart is overflowing with love. She wraps her arms around his shoulders and pulls herself closer to him. For a few seconds precious to Suzette, Victor does not move so that she can be close to him in his arms. Victor then walks across the room, past the double doors, and into the bedroom. Once at the side of the bed, he feels Suzette press her cheek into his. He waits a few seconds and then lowers her onto the bed. Suzette's arms anchor on to him.

"Good night, my dear Suzette," Victor says.

Suzette does not let go, and she says, "I am hurting. I need your warmth. I do not want to be away from your arms. My heart is overflowing with love. I ache for your touch. We do deeply care about each other; we do make beautiful love."

Suzette locks her eyes on his. Her emotional eyes look into the gray eyes she fell in love with over a century ago, and she says, "I cannot stop loving you."

Victor gently pulls her hands off him and kisses them. Her heart stops as he lets go of her hands and then straightens up. He then removes his tuxedo jacket, places it on the chair, and sits on the bed next to her. To her joy, he lifts her up into his arms, and then he gently pushes her head back, caresses her hair away from her neck, and begins to hungrily kiss her neck. Suzette wraps her arms around him. The emotional high from being in his arms as he kisses her neck makes her tremble with ecstasy as she begins to worry that he may just want to feed off her. He puts his hand under her chin and turns her to face him, and as his tender kiss becomes passionate, he gently lowers himself onto her. Victor passionately makes love to her, fulfilling her ever desire, except telling her that he loves her. His warmth is present; his affection and caresses overwhelm her heart. But her soul suffers in knowing that as his body makes love to her, his heart and thoughts are with Julieta.

Valentina wraps her satin robe around her. She tried to wait up for Victor, hoping he would come home early so she could talk to him. Groggy from lack of sleep, she starts to descend the stairs just as Victor makes his way to the stairs.

"Miss Santa Cruz?" Victor calls out to her as he removes his hat.

"It is you, Mr. Montenegro. I thought I heard Teo get up."

"Right, Miss Peterson went home after she put him to bed. I do not hear him. He will not venture in the dark; he will instead call out. Nevertheless, I will check on him. Thank you for watching over my nephew."

Valentina nods as she fights her sleepiness.

Victor contemplates her as the light of the moon streams over her. Her golden satin robe complements her dark hair, which is loosely resting on her shoulders. Victor is moved to protect her.

"It is not a good idea to be on the stairs in the dark," Victor says warmly.

"How was your evening?" Valentina asks.

"I thought of you," Victor declares.

Valentina looks down at him and stares, giving Victor the opportunity to admire her, and then she whispers, "You thought about me?"

"Yes."

"This must be a dream," Valentina laments.

"Why do you think you are dreaming?" Victor asks as he walks up the stairs to her.

"Mr. Montenegro would not have a reason to think of me when he is apart from me. Yes, this is a dream," Valentina says sadly.

Victor caresses her hair that survived the burn incident, and he gently asks her, "You really believe you are dreaming?"

"Yes, and I am beyond exhausted. I need rest. I shall control my dream. I will visualize the magnificent and charming Mr. Montenegro magically transporting me back to my bed," Valentina says.

Victor's hand holds up his walking stick and hat; his other hand waves over them, and they disappear. Feeling his warmth, Valentina's trembling hand caresses his chest, and then she gently presses her hand on his chest and says, "I can feel your heart beating, beating like a whole heart."

"I will escort you to your bed," Victor says, and then he lifts her up into his arms. Valentina exhales, overwhelmed with emotion from having him close to her. He respectfully carries her into her bedroom. At her bedside, he pauses for a minute and looks into her eyes, and then he says, "I did think about you. I am always thinking about you. He slowly lowers her onto her bed and covers her. He caresses her hair and says, "Good night."

Sunday morning, she wakes up feeling rested from sleeping in. Staring at the ceiling, she tries to decipher what happened the night before. The facts, as she remembers them, are that she fell asleep late, only to be startled awake, thinking that she heard Teo. She left her apartment to check on him. She feels that she must have confirmed that Teo was fine and went back to sleep, and then she dreamed of meeting Victor on the stairs. As she remembers his heart beating under her hand, she tells herself it was not real. She remembers the exhilarating feeling when Victor lifted her into his arms.

"Am I falling in love with Victor, or am I enchanted by everything that he represents?" Valentina ponders as a heaviness grows in her chest. She uncovers herself and discovers that she is wearing her robe.

With her heart still pounding from dashing out of the mansion, she walks through the cathedral doors, catches her breath, and makes the sign of the cross. She enters the soaring neo-Gothic church to thank God that she did not perish under a ton of stones. She will also ask for guidance for her confused heart. With her head bowed, she walks through the comforting peace toward the center pews. She stops, kneels down on one knee, and again makes the sign of the cross, and as she walks into the aisle, she looks up. Standing in front of a wrought-iron votive stand with all fifty candles lit is Victor. The image of candle flames from a smaller votive in front of him sway on his dark glasses as he caresses the two turtledoves he is cradling in his arm. Victor looks up, and he smiles at her.

Valentina walks through the aisle to him.

"Good afternoon, Miss Santa Cruz," Victor says, welcoming her.

"Good afternoon," Valentina whispers.

"Beautiful, aren't they?" Victor says as he caresses the turtledoves resting in the crook of his arm.

"Yes, they are," Valentina says as she slowly raises her hand.

Victor smiles to encourage her. As she lovingly caresses the turtledoves, Victor admires her over his sunglasses.

"What are their names?" Valentina asks.

"They are not my pets. When I entered, they were flying above the aisles. It was comforting to be greeted by them in my church. A dear late relative of mine loved turtledoves," Victor shares as he removes his glasses and hooks them onto the pocket of his dress jacket.

"I love turtledoves too because they symbolize love, and they mate for life," Valentina confirms as she strokes the birds.

"What symbolizes eternal love?" Victor asks.

Valentina looks up at him, and they lock eyes. Valentina can feel her heart in her throat. "Is eternal love possible?" she asks.

"I would like to believe it is," Victor admits.

"They have really taken to you," Valentina says, awestruck.

"I am good with animals," Victor says.

"The elements, illusions, magic, animals, diplomacy, treasure hunting, parenting—is there anything you find challenging?"

"Yes, I have a couple of challenges," Victor says as he gazes at her.

The clouds part, and the sun cascades through the seven huge arched stained-glass windows. The sun bathes the neo-Gothic church interior with the bright colors of the stained glass.

Victor puts his glasses back on. "I'll give you privacy. This is your home," Victor says warmly.

"And the turtledoves?"

"I am sure they will find their way home," Victor says.

He extends his arm out, and they both watch as the turtledoves take flight and fly around each other in the opal sunlight toward the highest point of the church and away from their view.

"Good afternoon, Miss Santa Cruz," Victor says, excusing himself.

Valentina walks to the middle of the pew, kneels down, and thanks God that Victor Montenegro was at the archaeology site to save her life. She also asks God to clarify what she feels for him.

Dr. Luque looks up from the file in his hand to the familiar knocking on his office's open door. "Good afternoon, Miss Laurant," he says.

"Please, call me Henrietta."

"How are you, Henrietta?"

"I am fine. I am in town to visit Victor, and I was wondering if you have any blood you can spare."

Dr. Luque walks to the refrigerator, and before he opens the door, he asks, "Would you like another jar for Mr. Ortiz?"

"Very kind of you to offer, but I will take care of Ivan."

Dr. Luque hands her the jar of blood.

"Here is my donation for your blood drives."

Dr. Luque takes the pouch of gold coins that Henrietta offers. "Very generous, thank you."

"You look great, Doctor. You have delicious, healthy glow," Henrietta teases.

"How is Drake Forester?" Dr. Luque asks.

"He is doing great. He does not know I am in town."

"Of course," Dr. Luque says.

Henrietta walks over to stand close to him, and she asks, "If I had a heart transplant, would I be able to enjoy mutual love?"

"Excellent question. I will explore that possibly, but I fear that your vampiric blood will corrupt your new heart."

"Dr. Luque, you are a handsome, intelligent, and great doctor, and the confidant of the town's most powerful man. But what makes you exceptional is that you have a whole heart. You need to spend less time in the lab and search for your true love."

"Thank you kindly. My practice is my vice and drive, and it would be unfair to her."

"I know you travel in the circles of immortal creatures who may not have the grace of God, but we do have eternal time. You must not forget that you are a mortal creature, for whom each day is a countdown to the last day of your life. If I was not madly in love with Ivan, I would fall in love with you," Henrietta says.

"You can always count on me for blood," Dr. Luque says.

Henrietta smiles seductively and moves in close to him, and she says, "Thank you, Doctor."

Dr. Luque smiles and steps back.

Henrietta says, "Although tempted, I will not bite you. I appreciate you. I respect your research, and I am grateful for the blood."

"I would be very grateful if you could give me a vial of Drake Forester's blood," Dr. Luque requests.

"On the next full moon, I will procure werewolf blood for you," Henrietta promises.

"I am very interested in Drake's blood specifically," Dr. Luque states.

"Why?"

"He is descended from a legendary werewolf lineage stretching back several centuries," Dr. Luque says.

"I will see what I can do. Drake does not believe in your science, and he has no interest in your research. However, I am fascinated by your intellect. What are you working on? A vaccine for longevity? Cell rejuvenation?"

"At this point, research and discovery," Dr. Luque says.

"Well, if you ever want to research firsthand what it feels like to have vampire blood in your veins, I will be happy to assist you. You would not be the first doctor to voluntarily infect himself in the name of research."

"I do not aspire to be a vampire, but thank you," Dr. Luque assures her.

Henrietta walks up close to Dr. Luque. "Thank you again," she says, holding the jar of blood close to her chest. She then leans into him and gives him a gentle kiss on the lips, and then she leaves his office.

Mrs. Walker informs Valentina that if she is free, Mr. Montenegro would appreciate her appearance in the library. Valentina rushes to the library, which causes her to almost collide with Dr. Luque at the open library door. Dr. Luque removes his hat and ushers her into the library. Valentina's excitement is crushed by the sight of Victor in the company of two other people.

"Miss Santa Cruz, thank you for coming. I would like to introduce you to my dinner guests."

As Valentina walks up to them, she feels a heaviness in the room. Ivan approaches her as Victor says, "Miss Valentina Santa Cruz is Teo's teacher. Valentina, this is Ivan Ortiz."

Ivan takes her hand and kisses it. "Lovely to meet you, Miss Santa Cruz," Ivan says. "Thank you for being Teo's teacher."

"Pleasure to meet you, Mr. Ortiz," Valentina says.

Valentina, uneasy with the energy she feels in the room, looks toward Victor.

Henrietta approaches her, and she puts her hands on Valentina's arms and kisses her on the cheeks as Victor says, "This is Henrietta Laurant."

"I am pleased to meet you, Miss Laurant."

Henrietta steps back, and she declares, "What a beautiful name, Valentina..." Henrietta looks at Victor, and then she clearly states, "Santa Cruz."

"Thank you," Valentina says.

Henrietta smiles at Valentina.

Dr. Luque lifts Henrietta's hand and kisses it, and he says, "You look lovely, Henrietta. How are you?"

"Thank you, Dr. Mario."

Victor walks over to stand next to Valentina and says, "Ivan Ortiz is my treasure-hunting partner and a good friend."

"How interesting," Valentina says.

"Yes, we go way back, a couple of centuries," Henrietta says with a laugh, and then she wraps her arm around Ivan's arm.

"They just arrived in town, and they and Mario will be having dinner here at the mansion. I do hope you will join us," Victor says.

"I would be delighted," Valentina says, not wanting to disappoint Victor.

"That will be charming. Victor tells us you are interested in anthropology—so fascinating," Henrietta says.

"Yes," Valentina says with a smile.

The party moves to the dining room.

"Please call Teo," Victor instructs the butler.

Teo follows his nanny into the dining room, holding tightly to her hand.

"Hello, precious love, how are you?" Henrietta asks.

"I am fine, madam, thank you. How are you?" Teo says.

"Oh my, you are quite a Montenegro. Charming. I am fine. Thank you for asking," Henrietta says.

Ivan walks up to him, and Teo, without letting go of his nanny's hand, shakes Ivan's.

"Good to see you, champ," Ivan says.

"Nice to see you, sir," Teo says.

Teo looks at the dining table and sees the extra plate sets. He then looks at Victor.

"May I please have dinner with my nanny in the kitchen?" Teo pleads.

"That is fine, son," Victor says in a sad tone that does not escape Valentina's ears.

"Thank you," Teo says, leading his nanny out of the dining room. They all wait for Teo to turn down the hall.

"That precious child still sees us as strangers. Either we need to visit more often, or you should think about relocating to New Orleans," Henrietta says as Ivan holds her seat.

"As he grows, he will warm up to you. He is surrounded by a lot of people who dote on him. I imagine it could be overwhelming to him," Victor says as he holds the chair for Valentina as she sits down.

As the men sit down, Henrietta says, "He should spend more time with Suzette. She is like a mother to him."

Dr. Luque notices that Valentina looks down at her gold plate, and a twinge of pain flashes on her face.

After the dinner, the party goes outside and sits in front of the famous Montenegro maze. The three men excuse themselves so that they can enjoy cigars a few feet away from Valentina and Henrietta, who are sitting at the wrought-iron table and are kept warm by heat lamps.

"Victor has shared with Ivan your passion for anthropology. Ivan, being a treasure hunter, finds that fascinating,"

Henrietta cups her hand over Valentina's hands, and she adds, "We all find it fascinating. I would love for us to make time to talk about nothing but ancient crypts."

Valentina looks at Victor's silhouette against the moonlight, and she smiles at the thought that he speaks of her to his friends.

Henrietta observes Valentina's loving gaze at Victor.

"How well do you know Victor?" Henrietta pries.

"I beg your pardon," Valentina replies.

"Has he shared any magic secrets with you?"

"No, he has not. But he has enchanted me with his magic on several amazing occasions."

Valentina looks toward Victor with warmth in her eyes, and she adds, "He saved my life."

"Is that right? How dreadful it must have been to be so close to death. What happened?"

"At an archaeological pit, he stopped a wall of stones from crushing me to death."

"How terrifying! I am glad Victor was there for you," Henrietta says, shuddering at the thought of being buried alive.

"Yes," Valentina responds. "I am so grateful."

"And so there they are, three souls discussing treasure hunting. It is a passion that Victor and Ivan share, and they have succeeded in locating jewels worth millions of dollars," Henrietta says as she strokes her hair into place.

The brilliance of the stones on her bracelet twinkle under the garden lights.

"That is such a beautiful bracelet. How old is it?" Valentina asks.

"Hundreds of years. It was part of a treasure that Ivan and Victor rescued from the sea," Henrietta says as she stretches her wrist in front of Valentina's admiring eyes.

"That is amazing!" Valentina says as she studies the bracelet.

"Amazing that it is hundreds of years old, or that it was part of a treasure, or that it is an absolutely beautiful piece?" Henrietta asks.

"All three!"

"Yes, I am spoiled. Instead of selling the jewelry for millions of dollars, he gives it to me. Beautiful sentiments from my love," Henrietta says.

Valentina smiles at Henrietta and says, "That is very touching."

"But I will admit that I am not the only woman he has given jewelry to. I would rather have Ivan donate all the jewelry to museums than have him give jewelry to someone who is not me," Henrietta gripes.

"Is that what Victor does, donate the jewelry to museums?"

"Yes, he donates the pieces to museums and charities or returns them to their country of origin. Victor is more excited by the hunt than by amassing a fortune from the treasures."

"He has never given jewelry to a woman?" Valentina inquires.

Henrietta caresses her bracelet and says, "The only woman to whom he gives jewelry is Suzette."

"Dr. Suzette Savarit?"

"Yes."

"A necklace?"

"No, earrings and a bracelet. He is a good man. He is a great parent and a great diplomat, and he cares about the citizens of Montenegro. I want him to be happy, and his happiness is with Suzette," Henrietta says.

Valentina sits up, and she inhales. The tightness in her chest is painful.

Henrietta smiles into her cup as she takes a small sip, and then she continues, "Suzette is madly in love with him."

"Is she?" Valentina asks as she feels her heart sink.

"Yes. It is not hard to fall in love with a man like Victor Montenegro. Heck, do not tell anyone, especially Suzette, but even I have a crush on Victor."

After the company departs, Valentina excuses herself and retires to her apartment. In her apartment, she fights the storms of emotions brewing all at once inside her as her mind clouds over with confusion. It frightens her that she suffered a painful reaction to hearing that the only woman upon whom Victor bestows legendary jewelry is a woman who happens to be madly in love with him. As she sits on her sofa, she tries to place her feelings. In the fog of confusion and conflicting feelings, there is one thing that is clear as water: in the core of her being, she feels she has a right to be in his life, a right that goes beyond being his nephew's teacher, a profound right that she feels does not need rhyme or reason. The pain in her heart turns into terror at the thought of not being part of his life. She scolds herself, "Stop being a child. Live your life. Do not live vicariously through Mr. Montenegro."

Since the first day she stepped into the Montenegro mansion, she has been welcomed by the man who is not just her employer, but a living legend, who enchants her and encourages her passions. He is not just present in her waking hours; he also lives in her dreams. She realizes that she has become addicted to Victor the person, the illusionist, the eccentric diplomat, and to his energy, which is mysterious but uplifting. She smiles and tells herself that perhaps she is just addicted to him and simply needs to wean herself from that addiction. Then her thoughts go to Suzette, and in her mind she sees her standing next to Victor, and she is stabbed with envy.

Her cell phone rings, and she answers.

"How are you, Valentina?" the caller asks, happy that she answered.

"I am well. How are you, Craig?" she says.

"Are you sure?" Craig Arquette asks.

"Yes."

"I just left a city function where one of the state's archaeologists told me that you were almost buried alive," Craig relays with worry.

"Right," Valentina confirms.

"I remember you telling me about your nightmares of getting buried alive," Craig says with concern.

"When Mr. Montenegro saved me, my fear that my nightmares might be prophetic stopped," Valentina says.

"I am grateful to Mr. Montenegro for saving you," Craig says.

"You are kind."

"I would love to see you, Valentina," Craig pleads.

"How about tomorrow night?" Valentina suggests.

"Yes, yes! There is a new restaurant in town I have been wanting to try, and I would love to take you."

"Fancy?" Valentina inquires.

"Very," Craig says, beaming with happiness.

"Sounds great," Valentina says.

"Do you want to meet at the restaurant, or can I come pick you up?" Craig says.

"Pick me up at the mansion," Valentina insists.

"Mr. Arquette," Victor says as he shakes his hand.

"How are you, Mr. Montenegro?"

"Fine, thank you. I am sorry, but do we have an appointment?" Victor asks his financial advisor.

"No. I am here to pick up Valentina."

"I see," Victor says.

Craig looks up the stairs and smiles. Victor looks up the stairs. Valentina walks down the stairs as both men admire how beautiful she looks in her red dress. In one hand she carries a clutch purse and silk shawl; her other hand glides down the rail as she makes her way down to them. She notices that both men are elegantly dressed in suits.

Craig extends his hand to her, and she lets go of the rail and holds on to his hand as her heels click down the last three stone stairs.

"Good evening," she says to them both.

"Good evening," they both reply.

"You look beautiful," Craig says.

"Thank you," Valentina says, letting go of his hand.

"I did not realize you had plans until I ran into Mr. Arquette," Victor says with a disappointed tone.

"Yes," Valentina confirms.

"I was on my way to call on you and invite you to an impromptu dinner and cocktail I will be hosting tonight for a small group of unexpected foreign dignitaries. But I see you have plans," Victor says.

"That is very thoughtful of you. Thank you just the same," Valentina says.

"Are you ready?" Craig asks.

"Yes," Valentina says as she hands him her shawl and turns around.

As Craig kindly drapes her shawl on her bare shoulders, Victor locks eyes with Valentina.

"Thank you," Valentina says to Craig as she pulls her eyes away from Victor's.

The butler informs Victor that his guests are arriving. Victor escorts Craig and Valentina out the door to greet his guests, who are slowly driving up the path. Craig, who had stationed his car close to the entry, moves ahead of Valentina to open the car door for her. A gust of wind blows across the path, taking with it Valentina's shawl. She turns around to see her shawl in Victor's hands. He approaches her and drapes the shawl over her bare shoulders as he says to her, "Enjoy your evening, and you are welcome to join me for a cocktail later tonight."

Valentina turns her head to look at him, and she smiles and says, "Thank you."

Victor steps away and walks toward his guests as Craig smiles at Valentina and helps her into his car.

Graveyard of the Pacific

Valentina returns to the mansion at midnight. The butler relays to her that although the guests have left, Mr. Montenegro is in the library, and if she is not tired, he would like to have a nightcap with her.

Valentina removes her shawl and hands the butler her shawl and purse.

She knocks on the library's open door. Victor looks away from the fireplace and smiles at her.

"You are home. How was your evening?" Victor says as he walks up to her.

"It was lovely. I decided I wanted to see a movie too. I am sorry I missed meeting your distinguished guests."

"They are all departing early in the morning for the other side of the world, so it had to be an early evening," Victor explains as he respectfully places his open hand on her lower back and escorts her to one of the Queen Anne chairs.

Valentina sits down as the butler enters. Victor sits down on the other Queen Anne chair across from her.

"What would you like to drink?" Victor asks as the butler waits.

"Cognac."

"Cognac, please," Victor instructs the butler.

"I appreciate you having a nightcap with me. There is something I would like to share with you," Victor says.

The butler brings a tray with a bottle of cognac and two tulip glasses filled with cognac.

Victor picks up the tulip glasses as he says to the butler, "Thank you. That is all for the evening. Good night."

Victor hands Valentina a tulip glass, raises his, and says, "To your health."

They both take a moment to savor the cognac.

"Excellent cognac, thank you," Valentina says.

"Tomorrow I depart for a couple of days. I discovered an old Spanish archive that my family kept over the centuries. It contains documentation about a Spanish galleon named *Dulce Alejandra* that was thrown off course by a storm and ran aground in the Columbia River—"

"The Columbia River!" Valentina says, alarmed.

"Yes," Victor confirms.

"That is the Graveyard of the Pacific, the most treacherous waters in the world," Valentina says with a worried tone.

"Yes, that mighty sandbar has devoured thousands of ships," Victor says.

Valentina stares at Victor with alarm in her eyes, and she asks, "Are you not afraid that it will devour you too?"

Victor sets his drink down on the table, and he tenderly looks at her and assures her, "Not in the least. We will have the most experienced crew in the world, a solid ship, and modern technology, and the shore is now equipped with lighthouses to help us navigate," Victor says calmly.

What Victor does not disclose to Valentina is that it will be a vampire crew, and as a vampire himself, there is no danger of him losing his life.

Valentina takes a sip of cognac and says, "I hope you are going to recover more than mission beeswax."

"Actually, the *Dulce Alejandra* was transporting mission beeswax. However, I discovered that what was forgotten to history is that the galleon was also carrying the lustrous treasure of a pirate ship that the crew of *Dulce Alejandra* found adrift, with no souls on board. On the pirate ship, they found a bounty of gold coins, diamonds, and colored jewels," Victor says.

"No souls aboard?" Valentina asks in disbelief.

"The sea is full of mysteries," Victor replies.

"I wish you a safe and successful treasure hunt," Valentina says in a feigned excited tone that does not mask her worry.

"Thank you," Victor says with a confident smile.

Valentina finishes her drink.

"Would you like another drink?" Victor asks, reaching for the bottle.

"No, thank you. I am bit tired," Valentina lies. She is excusing herself so that she will not keep Victor up and rob him of the rest he should get before venturing into the Graveyard of the Pacific.

Valentina stands up. Victor quickly stands up, walks her to the door, and opens it for her.

"Good night, Miss Santa Cruz."

"Good night, Mr. Montenegro. I look forward to hearing about your treasure hunt upon your safe return."

Victor smiles and says, "It will be a success. I will be back in a couple of days."

———

Two days later, Valentina is pacing the halls of the mansion. Victor has not returned from his hunt in the Graveyard of the Pacific, and she is doing her best not to imagine the worst. It is now late afternoon; shadows stretch against the walls. Valentina decides to go up to her apartment to take an aromatic bath to help calm her nerves. Valentina turns the corner, and she hears Henrietta cry out, "Destroy me! I cannot exist without my Ivan."

Valentina hurries to the stairs, where she sees the back of Henrietta as she sobs.

"Calm down, my dear," Dr. Luque says.

"Oh my God! What happened?" Valentina asks as she hurries to approach them.

Dr. Luque quickly pulls Henrietta into his arms, and as Henrietta cries into his black shirt, she pleads, "Where is he? I want to see him!"

"He is resting in a guest room," Mrs. Walker says as she walks down the stairs.

"Mrs. Walker, please escort Miss Laurant to see Mr. Ortiz," Dr. Luque requests.

"Wasn't Mr. Ortiz on the treasure hunt for the *Dulce Alejandra* with Mr. Montenegro?" Valentina asks in a panicked tone.

Ivan Ortiz and Maximus Flynt, who is a vampire werewolf, and three other vampires accompany Victor Montenegro on the treasure hunt in the Graveyard of the Pacific.

Ivan and Victor successfully locate the treasure, which the crew hoists onto their ship, making sure not one brilliant stone is left behind, and they also collect the mission beeswax. As they depart in high spirits with the legendary jewels and historical mission beeswax, in the Graveyard of the Pacific, Victor's ship crosses paths with the ship of the exalted werewolf Drake Forester and his crew of werewolves.

"Timely and poetic," Drake bellows to them from his deck.

"How so?" Victor demands.

"First, allow me to thank you in advance for your search for and hoisting up of the *Dulce Alejandra*'s treasure," Drake says, laughing.

"The audacity of that creature to think—"

Drake interrupts Ivan and says, "No. Do not get confused. My mission here is to destroy you, Ivan Ortiz. The treasure will become my reward for dispatching you and your ghoulish friend Victor Montenegro to hell."

Drake then looks at the crew and says to them, "I find it poetic that your immortality will end in the Graveyard of the Pacific."

Victor laughs and says, "Sail away, or this will be your watery grave."

"I will let you and your dark crew leave with your lives if you hand me the chest with the jewels and Ivan Ortiz's head in it," Drake bargains.

"You are an idiot, Forester. Henrietta cannot, nor will she ever, love you—not as long as you are in love with her. Destroying me will not change the fact that you will never share mutual love with her or any other vampiressas. It is an inconvenient truth that you and your hairy pals continuously ignore as you all seek the love of our vampiressas," Ivan chastises him.

"How are you planning to destroy a crew of vampires?" Victor mocks.

As Drake's ship moves closer to Victor's, he and his crew of werewolves pull out silver swords.

The vampires smirk as they look at one another.

"You suckers take issue with the fact that the lovely vampiressas prefer werewolf blood to your rodent-laced blood," Drake mocks.

"Turn your ship around, and take with you what is more valuable to you all—your lives," Victor orders.

"You hear that, men? Victor is being charitable because he does not bite," Drake says, and then he and his crew laugh. "You do not fool me, illusionist. You believe that if you do not destroy a creature, the gates of heaven will open up to you. I almost feel pity for you."

"Get the hell out of here, Forester!" Maximus warns.

"Shut your fangs, traitor. We welcomed you, a cursed werewolf, into our community, and you decided to lower yourself to second-class status by willfully becoming the enemy," Drake yells.

"If chitchat is what you want, we can arrange to meet on the next full moon. I will bring the rum," Ivan dismisses.

Drake rams his sword through the fog and says, "It burns me that after so many decades, Henrietta still runs to you, and you receive her with open arms. I want to enjoy the last two centuries of my life knowing that she will never run to your arms again because I destroyed you."

Drakes looks at Victor's vampire crew and says to them, "With our silver swords, we will spill the damned blood of each and every one of you, unanchor your souls from your wretched bodies, and toss them to hell."

The crew bursts into laughter.

Victor says to Ivan, "We should get swords like theirs, with monster-friendly wooden handles that are bewitched to only be held by their owners."

Then Victor says to Drake, "If you were a true gentleman, you would have challenged us to a duel and given us the courtesy to select our weapons. Fortunate for us, an enslaved human in your community warned us of your plot, and we come prepared."

The sound of semiautomatic rifles coming out of hiding and flying into the hands of the vampires gets the attention of Drake and his aghast crew.

"These rifles are loaded with pure silver bullets. Your swords are not a match for the speed of our bullets," Ivan says, pointing his rifle between Drake's eyes.

Drakes throws his sword down and jumps onto the deck of Victor's ship. He stands facing Ivan and challenges him, "Fight me like a man."

Drake's men lower their swords.

Victor's men keep their rifles pointed at Drake and his crew as Ivan hands his rifle to Maximus.

"I do not want a murder on my hunt to curse me. If you want to fight to the death, do it on another day," Victor says as he holds his rifle steady, aimed between Drake's eyes.

An eerie splashing in the calm waters calls their attention, and then they are all overcome by a high-pitched sound coming from the ocean. A blinding flash causes them to lose sight momentarily.

After their eyes have readjusted to the darkness, they see that Drake is no longer on board and that he, his ship, and his crew have vanished.

"The Graveyard of the Pacific has claimed another crew," Maximus ventures.

"I am freezing…" Ivan says.

"Freezing? He had my blood boiling," Victor fumes.

"Burning pain," Ivan complains as he puts his hand on his side.

"You are bleeding, brother," Victor says.

Ivan lifts his shirt up, revealing a deep slash that slowly closes. But the cut does not heal with new skin; instead, there is a thick scar.

"That son of a bitch had a silver dagger, and he branded you," a crew member says.

"Drake wants to make sure the scar will be a constant reminder of his contempt for you," Maximus says.

"Ivan suffered an injury during the hunt. It is a superficial cut, and he will be fine," Dr. Luque explains to Valentina.

"Is Mr. Montenegro fine? Where is Mr. Montenegro, Doctor?" Valentina begs.

"I am right here, Miss Santa Cruz," Victor announces.

Valentina turns around and sees Victor; she rushes to him and hugs him. Victor hugs her back as Dr. Luque observes their warm embrace.

"Mr. Ortiz's injury had Miss Laurant in tears, and I feared that you too had been hurt," Valentina says as she slowly pulls away from his arms to look at him.

"Thank you for your concern. The only one who got hurt was Ivan. Fortunately, one of the men on the crew is a doctor, and Ivan is now in the good hands of Mario," Victor says.

"I am not dying," Ivan comforts Henrietta as she weeps inconsolably on his chest.

"I swear to you, love of my life, that I had no clue Drake was planning to ambush you in the Graveyard of the Pacific," Henrietta says, sobbing.

"I believe you. He wants to destroy me so he can have you all to himself. There is no doubt that he loves you. A mad love, but love nonetheless," Ivan says.

"I will never see him again," Henrietta promises.

"No. I am not asking you to walk away from a man who loves you. I know he treats you like a queen. He just wants me destroyed. I have no right to tell you what to do with your personal life. I will only intervene if I feel you are in danger. He will not hurt you because he does not want to lose you. But, I will tell you this: next time I see that half of a man, one of us will die."

"No! No! I will see to it that you and Drake never cross paths again."

"Well, that beast is clever. He sought me out in treacherous waters, armed with enchanted swords and passionate about destroying me. Unbeknownst to him, one of their enslaved humans told Agnes of his plan, and Agnes warned Maximus. Thus, he did not count on us having rifles with silver bullets. Still, he had a backup plan to attack me and scar me for life, while having a witch or demon distract us and blind us to help them escape before we could fire our rifles."

Henrietta holds him tightly as she cries out, "It pains me deeply that my love for you has made you suffer."

"Suffer? Suffer how? My dear, it was just nick," Ivan soothes her.

"He scarred you," Henrietta mourns.

"Actually, I like the scar. It reminds me that I was once human. Victor is fine. The whole crew is fine. Please, do not call Suzette and tell her what happened," Ivan says.

Henrietta's sobs grow louder.

Ivan tilts her chin up and showers her with kisses, and then he lets her go. He walks to the dresser, and without saying a word, he walks back to her and gently places a crown of diamonds, rubies, and emeralds on her head.

"Well, pardon me, I will check on Ivan," Dr. Luque says, excusing himself.

"Thank you, Mario," Victor says.

Victor turns to look at Valentina, who is still a bit shaken.

"We are all fine, Miss Santa Cruz," Victor says with a warm smile.

"Just the thought that you—"

"Yes?" Victor asks attentively.

"I am happy that you are all fine," Valentina says with a smile.

"Do you have a minute?" Victor asks.

"Yes, of course."

"Follow me to the library, please, Miss Santa Cruz."

As they walk toward the library, Victor asks, "How is the investigation going at the Richardson estate?"

"Interesting developments. It is an old burial site and a crime scene. They exhumed bodies in coffins from the turn of the century, and they discovered bodies buried on top of the old coffins with modern articles of clothing," Valentina shares.

"Turn of the century," Victor says sadly as he remembers Julieta.

"Yes, it is very sad. But I am not surprised that the burial site dates back to the turn of the century," Valentina says.

"Why do you say that?" Victor asks.

"Because after you saved me from being buried by stones, I had a dream that I was buried under bricks, and when I was pulled out from the mountain of bricks, I looked down and saw that I was wearing an Edwardian dress."

Victor comes to a halt. He turns to face her and questions, "Edwardian dress?"

"Yes, a turn-of-the-century dress."

"Turn of the century; bricks," Victor repeats as he studies Valentina.

"Yes, Mr. Montenegro."

"Must have been a dreadful dream," Victor laments.

"I was more intrigued that I was wearing a turn-of-the-century dress than being buried alive," Valentina says.

"I am sorry you experienced such a dream," Victor says with regret.

Valentina can hear the sadness in Victor's words and see in his eyes that her dream touched him.

Victor escorts her into the library. On the library table sits a long wooden box. Valentina, in awe, walks to stand in front of it.

"*Dulce Alejandra?*"

"Yes," Victor says proudly.

Victor slowly lifts the wooden lid of a modern trunk holding centuries-old treasure. The trunk is brimming with every jewel known to man. The clean luster of the stones conceals the fact that they laid at the bottom of the Graveyard of the Pacific for centuries.

Valentina stares at the treasure with amazement.

"I had my jewelers clean the brilliant stones and jewelry. It took a team of jewelers an entire day to restore them to their glory. It is hard to imagine that such brilliant jewels were rescued from an abandoned ship and then dragged down in the *Dulce Alejandra* to the bottom of the sea," Victor says.

"It is incredible! Such beautiful jewels, with a rich history dating back for centuries. May I touch them?" Valentina says, enthralled.

"Cup your hands together, please," Victor instructs.

Victor showers her cupped hands with loose gems of assorted colors and diamonds.

Valentina studies the brilliant stones as she marvels over the weight of the historical jewels.

Victor contemplates her as she looks at the beautiful jewels, spellbound by their beauty. After a few seconds, Victor cups her hands with his. Valentina looks up at him, and their eyes lock. Victor warmly gazes into her eyes as he gently closes her hands together with his hands. His hands hug her hands for a few seconds. Victor then tenderly smiles at her and lets go of her hands. Valentina opens her hands, and resting on her cupped palms is a beautiful gold necklace with a hundred diamonds and rubies. Valentina is awestruck into silence.

"A necklace I rescued from the Graveyard of the Pacific," Victor says. He then gently lifts up the necklace from her trembling hands. The brilliance, beauty, and rarity of the necklace dazzle her. Victor gently drapes the necklace on her, and he leans in to latch the clasp behind her neck. The excitement of the brilliant necklace is replaced by the electrical charge in her heart from having him close enough to share a kiss. Victor slowly pulls back, and he admires her for a moment. Victor then materializes a mirror out of the air, and he holds it up for Valentina. Valentina's shaking hand caresses the beautiful necklace.

"It is a beautiful necklace befitting a queen," Valentina says as she gazes at the reflection of the sparkling jewels on her neck.

"Yes," Victor agrees.

He smiles at her and says, "The necklace is yours."

Valentina looks away from the mirror and studies him, and then she says, "I beg your pardon?"

"I want you to have the necklace," Victor says.

"It is incredibly beautiful, timeless, and priceless. I cannot accept it," Valentina says.

Victor throws the mirror into the air, and it vanishes.

Valentina raises her hands to remove the necklace from her neck.

Victor stops her hands with his and says to her, "Because it is incredibly beautiful, timeless, and priceless, I want you to have it."

Stunned, Valentina does not pull her hands away from his. She can feel the necklace cling to her chest every time she breathes in. Speechless, she studies his eyes.

"See it as a token of my appreciation for your passion for anthropology and my immense gratitude that Teo treasures you as a teacher," Victor says as he slowly lowers her hands.

Valentina lets him hold her hands as she captures the moment. His presentation, words, and tone not only order but move Valentina to accept the necklace. She timidly smiles with gratitude.

"Thank you, truly, thank you," she says, overwhelmed by his

generous and touching gift.

"When I pulled it up from the sea and held it up to the light, I could not imagine anyone else owning it but you," Victor admits.

"I must confess that I have never received a gift as significant as this beautiful necklace."

"Significant?" Victor asks.

"You could have died in the pursuit of this necklace, and I was afraid you would. I am very grateful and relieved that you did not perish in that godforsaken sea. I will forever treasure this gift," Valentina says, her eyes watering.

Victor tenderly smiles at her.

Valentina holds back her desire to hug Victor in the private library by gently pressing her hands on the necklace.

The knock on the library door interrupts them.

"Come in," Victor says.

Dr. Luque walks in. He notices how Victor and Valentina are lovingly contemplating each other.

"Good afternoon," he says.

"Good afternoon," Valentina says, turning to look at Dr. Luque. She looks back at Victor and says sweetly, "Thank you."

She looks at the doctor, and then she says to them both, "Excuse me."

The doctor notices the necklace on Valentina as she leaves the library, and he waits to hear the door close before he asks Victor, "How is your heart?"

"Broken," Victor reminds him.

"A broken heart will not bestow priceless jewelry on a woman; that is what a whole heart does," Dr. Luque reasons.

"A beautiful necklace like that deserves to be worn by a beautiful woman, not locked up in a museum," Victor explains.

"Suzette is beautiful," Dr. Luque says.

"And your point is?" Victor asks, confused, as he sits in front of the trunk and caresses the jewels.

"You did not give the necklace to Suzette, with whom you have a history spanning over a century. You did not think to give the necklace to one of the countless beautiful women who flock to you to be enthralled by your magic. You gave the necklace to Miss Santa Cruz," Dr. Luque points out.

"Miss Santa Cruz is beautiful," Victor reasons.

"Victor, you are in love with Valentina," Dr. Luque states.

Victor opens a black velvet bag, into which he pours many gems and a necklace. He pulls the strings to close the bag, hands the bag to Dr. Luque, and directs, "This is an order. Find your true love, and when you do, give her the necklace. I feel terrible that you are always on call, and when you are not on call, you are in the lab trying to find the elixir that will grant me mutual love."

"Is that why you are afraid to admit it?" Dr. Luque says.

"Admit what?"

"You will not admit to yourself that you are in love with her so that you will not have to deal with the pain that she will never love you."

"I want her to be as free as a turtledove so she can find her mutual love," Victor says.

"In your denial, the moments you two have shared must have escaped you. I have been present when your souls connected through each other's eyes. I have felt the chemistry between the two of you. The embraces you two shared were warm and profound. From my observations, it is not love that she feels, but I can see that she is infatuated with you. She is enamored with your charisma, your mysterious aura, and your dedication to those you care about. If I can pick up on the chemistry between you two, I am sure she does as well. My guess is that she is in her apartment admiring her necklace, and her female intuition is confirming that such a beautiful necklace from a man—"

"In time," Victor interrupts, "she will see that her feelings will not grow deeper. She will remain at the border of love, where she will feel only chemistry, affection, and attraction for me. My fear is that she will go insane with confusion as to why her affection for me does not blossom into love," Victor laments.

"Well, prepare yourself, as you unwillingly opened the door. You could tell her a thousand and one reasons why, outside of love, you gave her a necklace of immense historical and monetary value, but she will know in her soul that there is one, and only one, reason you gave her that necklace, and that is out of love. She is not blind. If I can see the love in your eyes for her, so does she. Whether your heart is ready or not, that sentimental gift welcomed her into your heart, where she will explore all of your secrets."

A guttural laughter booms throughout the library. Victor stands up as Dr. Luque looks at him, aghast.

Dark smoke tunnels out of the fire in the fireplace. As Victor and Dr. Luque watch, the dense, dark smoke morphs into a creature with the body of a man dressed like a pirate from the sixteenth century, but with a hideous face resembling a disfigured boar, with two long tusks with flames on the tips.

"A demon in disguise," Victor says to Dr. Luque.

"You are not welcome here, demon," Victor scolds.

"Well, I got tired of waiting for an invitation, and you and I have a pending matter. So here I am," the demon mocks.

"There is no pending matter. Leave! To hell with you!"

The demon walks to the trunk, and his gloved hand swims in the jewels as he says, "Man can tap into the energy of the universe and be moved to create music, art, and literature that evoke and provoke all the human senses that one can feel. A song, a painting, a passage in a book—these have the power to make people laugh, cry, lust, feel indignant, feel happy, or just escape. Notice that I did not say love? Because no matter how beautiful the melody is, how impressive the painting may be, or how profound the words of a book's passage are, these will never touch a heart to love."

The demon looks at Dr. Luque. "Science limits you, Doctor. The art of science will never create an artificial heart that will feel true mutual love. I say forget about Montenegro's heart; you do not have a prayer," the demon ridicules.

Dr. Luque cannot tear his eyes away from the hideous creature. Adrenaline has his body on alert, and he feels an indescribable fear and utter contempt for the demon, but his mind struggles to rationalize what he is seeing in order to react.

The demon laughs with relish at Dr. Luque, silenced by fear.

The demon looks at Victor and says, "Your pious sister devoted decades of her life to prayer for a miracle to make your heart whole again and to save your soul, and instead of an answer to her prayers, she winds up dead in a church. Now, that is poetic enough to move even me," the demon says with a laugh.

"You did not come here to talk about art, emotions, and my sister. Why in the hell is a condemned beast like you in my home?" Victor demands.

"Tsk, tsk, you are not being diplomatic," the demon mocks. "Why am I here? Right—to give you a friendly reminder: your soul is still the property of the devil," the demon says as he commands the wooden lid to crash down on the chest of jewels.

"Stay out of my home! You and your evil brethren are never welcome in my home. This is not hell; you do not have any right to occupy space in my home," Victor says angrily.

The demon's laughter storms around them.

"I am feeling generous. I could not help but overhear. I lie. Overhearing is a habit we often indulge in."

"Must be the only indulgence you have a right to," Dr. Luque spits out.

"Look who found his balls to talk," the demon says.

The demon looks back at Victor and says, "Since you are the property of the devil, we strive to make you as miserable as possible. We feed off suffering. And we learned that you are very sentimental and that you suffer greatly when you lose love. You suffered over Clara. You suffered even more over Julieta. And you will suffer even greater still over Valentina, for the same reasons you suffered over Julieta."

Victor stares at the demon. The demon laughs at him, walks into the fireplace, tips his tricorn hat, and vanishes. As the heat from the fireplace sends out the rotting stench of the demon, Dr. Luque demands, "What in God's name was that?"

"It was a demon from hell," Victor says bitterly.

"Are you telling me demons exist?" Dr. Luque argues.

"Mario, you are asking a vampire if a demon exists," Victor points out.

Dr. Luque goes to the bar and pours them both shots of tequila, puts the bottle of tequila under his arm, and hands Victor a shot. They both take two shots of tequila, and then Victor questions, "What did he mean by saying that I would suffer for the same reasons?"

"Father of lies!" Dr. Luque recalls. "Do not listen to that thing; he was lying to manipulate you."

"That was a threat," Victor says.

"How do you mean?"

"They want me to suffer. They want me to feel that I am hopeless and just lay down and die."

"You are suffering because you are condemned, and your heart is cursed," Dr. Luque says.

"After so many decades since the day the demon dog attacked me, evil decided to make an appearance in my home. Why?" Victor asks.

"It could only be for two reasons, I believe. Either you are on the cusp of being freed, and the dark forces want you to believe otherwise, or you are still condemned, and they just want to torment you by puzzling you."

"The timing is also peculiar," Victor says.

"Let's not give it another thought," the doctor eagerly suggests.

"My suffering will be greater…"

Dr. Luque stares at Victor, confused.

"I am already suffering from unrequited love with Valentina," Victor says.

"It took a demon to make you admit it," Dr. Luque gripes.

The blood rushes to Victor's face, and he says, "That is it! I am in love. Love does not dwell in hell. Mutual love or not, I can still love. My suffering is less because I am in love, and they are not happy about that."

"Did they come calling when you fell in love with Julieta?" Dr. Luque asks.

"No."

"Why now with Valentina?" Dr. Luque wonders out loud.

"Good question," Victor says, fraught with intrigue.

"Could Valentina be the key to your salvation?" Dr. Luque asks.

"Perhaps. Or the key to my greater suffering," Victor says.

"How so?" Dr. Luque asks with incredulous eyes.

"Valentina is in danger because I am in love with her," Victor says, troubled.

End of Book 2

The Montenegro Saga continues in Book 3 of the series in which Suzette, Victor, Valentina, Henrietta, along with new mystical creatures, will continue their journey of forbiddance as they battle for true love in their macabre worlds.

CPSIA information can be obtained
at www.ICGtesting.com
Printed in the USA
BVOW08*0841211116
468476BV00003B/9/P